Alex Obviously Wanted Her.

He hadn't gone out of his way to hide his desire for her. Or his distrust. A distrust he had every reason to feel. She silently cursed Damon for putting her in this position, but she was as much to blame for perpetuating the lie.

She gazed into his eyes. She was free to tell him the truth and then they could move on with their relationship. Why did she hold back?

She would only be here until the end of the week. Did she really want to get in any deeper? Could she stop herself? If her feelings for him were purely physical, she could deal with an affair. But her emotions were becoming involved. Alex touched her in a place no one had been able to reach before.

Her heart.

And it frightened her more than she cared to admit.

Dear Reader

Welcome to October's sizzling line-up for Desire™. And we're delighted to bring you another wonderful novel from best-selling author Diana Palmer. In *Callaghan's Bride*, our **Man of the Month**, rugged bachelor Callaghan Hart, has no intention of getting married—but can innocent Tess Brady tempt him otherwise? And in *The Best Husband in Texas*, Austin Farrell is determined to prove that he is the best—and only—husband for Iris Smith!

This month, there are also two very unusual marriage proposals. Faith Kolanko can't believe Jared Whitewolf's offer—a home, a baby and *him* in return for saying 'I do!' in the latest story from Sara Orwig. And continuing the **Bachelor Battalion** series, Donna Candello finds herself becoming *The Oldest Living Married Virgin* when she agrees to marry Sergeant Jack Harris to save her reputation.

To complete the line-up, there's the first in a fantastic new mini-series, **Outlaw Hearts**, from Cindy Gerard, and a fun pretend-fiancée story from Kathryn Taylor.

Happy reading!

The Editors

The Forbidden
Bride-To-Be

KATHRYN TAYLOR

SILHOUETTE
DESIRE

*Silhouette, Silhouette Desire and Colophon
are registered trademarks of Harlequin Books S.A.,
used under licence.*

*First published in Great Britain 1999
Silhouette Books, Eton House, 18-24 Paradise Road,
Richmond, Surrey TW9 1SR*

© Kathryn Attalla 1998

ISBN 0 373 76182 1

22-9910

*Printed and bound in Spain
by Litografía Rosés S.A., Barcelona*

KATHRYN TAYLOR

has a passion for romance novels that began in her late teens and left her with an itch to discover the world. After living in places as culturally diverse as Athens, Greece, and Cairo, Egypt (where she met and married her own romantic hero), she returned to the U.S.A., and she and her husband settled in the quiet village of Warwick, New York. Kathryn says, 'Although my writing allows my mind to soar in the clouds, I have an energetic eleven-year-old who keeps my feet planted on the ground.'

Other novels by Kathryn Taylor

Silhouette Desire®

Taming the Tycoon

For my critique partner, Karen,
to whom I owe an enormous debt of gratitude.

Prologue

A light wind rustled the black lace curtains at the door, causing the candles to flicker. Sophie Anders adjusted the shawl on her shoulders. Golden threads shimmered in the candlelight. The heavy scent of sandalwood incense tickled her nostrils and she had to stifle a sneeze.

The carousel's Wurlitzer organ piped out a hauntingly familiar song on the midway. She raked a handful of curls back from her face and smiled at the handsome man sitting in the folding chair across from her. "Why do you want to introduce me to your family as your fiancée? We're not even dating."

Damon Winston grinned sheepishly. "The family is nagging me about getting married, so I sort of told them I had a fiancée."

She glanced down at her white peasant blouse and

red swirling skirt. "And I'm the best you could come up with? They'll never buy it."

"Actually, you're the worst I could come up with, and I don't want them to buy it. I want them to oppose it."

"Why, thank you." She punched his shoulder in mock exasperation.

"You know I didn't mean that as an insult. To my family, a nonconformist is someone who wears white after Labor Day. You would be an alien being."

Sophie knew better than to be insulted. She had worked for Damon while in college, and their friendship had begun in part due to their mutual enjoyment of taunting each other. She credited their enduring relationship to the fact that she had never gotten romantically involved with him.

"Why don't you just tell them you don't want to get married? I, for one, would vouch for your poor character—fidelity not being one of your strongest suits."

"Come on, Sophie. I've never asked you for anything."

"What about all those double shifts you had me pull at the restaurant?"

Damon gave her one of those charming smiles that usually had the ladies falling at his feet. "Besides that."

"How about the time you set me up on a blind date with your college pal, Octopus Man?"

"After one date with you, he decided to be a priest."

"Or the time you asked me to pick you up at the airport and left me waiting two hours because you

had made a short detour with one of the steward-
esses.''

"Okay. I get the point. But this is absolutely the
last favor I will ever ask of you. No one will get
hurt.''

Sophie lowered her head. Some Gypsies would
think her crazy for hesitating. Running scams might
be part of Romany heritage, but not a part her family
had cultivated. "I don't know, Damon. I'd planned
to work the carnival over my vacation. The youth
center needs money for art supplies...."

He groaned in frustration. "How many times have
I told you, you won't get rich by working for free?''

"I didn't get rich working for you, either,"
she jokingly shot back. "That's why I'm self-
employed.''

Damon had never understood why she volunteered
her time teaching art classes at the youth center. She
received so much more than she gave those kids.
Wealth had different meanings for different people.
To him, the measure would always be monetary.

He lifted the tarot card and turned it facedown on
the table. "Are the paying customers really fooled
by this Gypsy act you put on.''

"The carnival is for charity. And it's not an act.
I'll admit that I don't have the talent my mother does,
but I get really strong impressions about people.''

"I'll make a deal with you. Do this for me and
I'll donate two thousand dollars to the center.''

Her eyes widened. "Two thousand dollars?'' Although her first instinct was to decline the offer, she
thought about all the things the center could do with
the money and she found her resolve wavering. What

harm could there be in playing the part of an unsuitable fiancée for a few days?

"And you'd get an exciting, fun-filled vacation, all expenses paid to beautiful Fairfield, Connecticut."

The evening sky crackled with heat lightning. Was it a sign she should go, or a warning to stay away? *Get a grip, Sophie. It was a quirk of nature.* "There is no such thing as a free ride, Damon."

He twisted his fingers together until his knuckles cracked. "Jeez. You sound like Alex."

"Who's Alex?"

"My stepbrother."

That Damon had never mentioned a stepbrother in the four years she had known him should have been enough to send up the alarm bells. "I don't know...."

He arched his eyebrow. "You'll be doing it for charity."

"All right," she found herself saying despite her misgivings. Gooseflesh covered her skin. She glanced down at the intersecting lines on her palm. Was this the crossroad her mother had predicted in her future?

One

Sophie gaped at the walled fortress. The stone watchtower at the entrance added to her growing apprehension. A brass plate near the wrought-iron gate read The Sanctuary, and beyond the iron bars the massive house loomed in the distance. What had she gotten herself into?

Droplets of rain blurred the windshield. How fitting, she thought. The gray fog, nearly obscuring the gables, lent a haunting ambience to the entire scene before her.

She turned toward Damon. His lips curved upward in what she could only describe as a sneer. He locked his fingers in a death grip over the steering wheel of the Porsche. She barely recognized him as the same unflappable man who breezed though life on his charming smile.

"It ain't much, but it's home," he muttered sarcastically. Obviously The Sanctuary wasn't a haven to him.

As she returned her gaze to the sprawling estate, she realized just how little she knew about Damon. Not enough to decipher his true motives for this charade. His anxiety didn't jive with a man who only wanted his well-meaning, if interfering, family off his case about marriage.

"Tell me a little about your family."

His eyes narrowed suspiciously. "Why?"

"We're supposed to be engaged. Shouldn't I know a little about your life?" He'd never mentioned growing up on an estate the size of a convention center. What else had he left out?

He paused in thought, then shrugged. "You're right, of course. My mother is a typical mother. She wants me married off to a nice girl so I can give her a pack of grandchildren."

"And your brother?"

"*Step*brother," he corrected with a slight edge to his voice. He inhaled deeply and relaxed in the bucket seat. "Alex is…intense. He was kidnapped when he was young, and his father paid a fortune to get him back. But don't mention it. He *never* talks about the incident."

Although stories of kidnapping were romanticized among the Gypsies, she could only imagine the scars an incident like that left behind. Again, she wondered why Damon had never mentioned his stepbrother.

"Are the two of you close?"

"Not exactly." He jammed the car into gear and drove up the long driveway. Clearly anything else she wanted to ask would have to wait.

They were met at the foot of the flagstone steps

by a butler. He opened her door, then strode around the car to open Damon's door.

"Welcome home, Master Damon. I hope you had a good trip." The man's formality forced Sophie to swallow a laugh.

"Thank you, William." Damon took her arm and led her through the misty rain into the house.

Her heels clicked against the marble floor of the large foyer. A crystal chandelier that suspended from the cathedral ceiling shimmered brightly. Feeling hopelessly out of place, she smoothed her ruffled skirt. Now she understood how her ancestors felt when they'd been summoned to the castles of Europe to provide entertainment for the nobility.

"Why didn't you warn me?" she muttered angrily.

"I didn't want you to come rehearsed, ready to play a part."

"Isn't that what I'm doing?"

"Yes. But I wanted the estate to take you by surprise. No preconceived notions."

Apparently there was more to Damon's scheme than he'd led her to believe. He was playing with her, too, and she wasn't up to his kind of games. She had agreed to act as his fiancée as long as the small deception hurt no one.

William joined them, preventing her from further questioning. "I'll have the bags taken to your rooms. Your mother is at the club. She'll be back for dinner."

"And Alex?" Damon asked.

"At the stables, I believe."

"I better go tell him I'm here. Make yourself at home." Damon placed an obligatory kiss on her cheek. "The living room is down the hall to the right and the library to the left. If you get lost, don't worry. It will only take a search party a few hours to find you in this place."

She plastered on a smile and pretended to be amused. "Hurry back, dear."

Left on her own, Sophie made a slow pirouette to survey the foyer again. So opulent, so elegant, so sterile. The sheer size of the place might give the illusion of space, but she felt as restricted as if she had been locked in a closet. Would she be able to survive an entire week?

Alexander Sinclair kicked the dirt from his boot and stepped into the kitchen. He glanced at his watch. Lunch would have to wait if he wanted to shower and change before his brother arrived. He grabbed an apple from the counter and bit into the crunchy fruit.

If nothing else, his vacation would be interesting this year. Damon was planning to get married? That remained to be seen. His brother enjoyed his freedom too much to settle down without major incentive. Was his intended a wealthy socialite? Or was something else behind his decision to marry a woman he'd never mentioned before last week? Alex had been curious enough to come home and find out.

As he started down the hall, he saw a familiar-looking woman enter the library. He withdrew into the shadows. A knot formed in his stomach. He could have sworn he'd stepped into the past. What was going on?

Convinced that the lighting had played tricks on him, he continued down the hall. The faint sound of music floated on the air. Three suitcases at the foot of the stairs let him know Damon and his guest had arrived.

The soft strains of Bizet's *Carmen* became louder as he reached the archway that led to the library. A pair of red leather pumps had been discarded just inside the room. Beneath the bay window a woman swayed enticingly to the violin music. A small cassette player was hooked to a wide black belt that emphasized her narrow waist, and a kelly green skirt swirled around long shapely legs. Her mane of dark curls lifted as she swung her head in a circular motion. This time the tightening in his body occurred several inches lower than his stomach.

Her seductive dance picked up with the tempo. She spun across the highly polished floors as if aware of every piece of furniture even though her eyes were closed. He was drawn to her face. Again he noticed distinct similarities. Only this woman lacked any inhibition, unlike Marie.

Marie. He hadn't thought of her in years. What cruel plan did Damon have in mind this time? Alex refused to believe that this woman's resemblance to his ex-fiancée was mere coincidence.

He heard a gasp. A pair of startled green eyes locked on him a split second before she slammed full force into him. Instinctively he grabbed her waist as he stumbled backward into the wall.

For a stunned moment he could neither think nor feel. Slowly his senses returned. Short, panting breaths caressed his neck, wreaking havoc with his hormones. The scent of strawberry engulfed him. Her full round breasts brushed over his chest as she fumbled with the off button of her cassette player. He was sure she felt him grow hard.

"I'm sorry," she muttered.

"No harm." In fact, he enjoyed the feeling of her snuggled against him a little too much.

"How long have you been here?"

He laughed. "Long enough to catch the show."

Her embarrassed moan reverberated against his chest. As she shook her head, her silky hair brushed over his cheek. "Leather."

"Excuse me?"

"You smell like leather."

"Sorry." He dropped his hands from her waist.

She took a step back and smiled. "Don't apologize. It's a nice scent." She smoothed her clothes, then extended her hand. "You must be Alex. Damon has told me so much about you."

Was it his imagination, or had she winced at her words? "He mentioned nothing about you," he said as he enclosed her delicate hand in his. He felt her tremble slightly.

"Oh, well, I'm Sophie." A healthy blush covered her cheeks. She smoothed the mass of ringlets that surrounded her face like a halo. "Damon went to the stables to look for you."

"He missed me."

"Apparently."

During the long pause that followed, he stared at her, but she remained steady under his gaze. Damn, she was beautiful.

"Nice place you have here."

"You think so?"

"Not really." She closed her eyes and sighed. "Oh, jeez, I did it again."

Alex grinned at her honesty. ''The Sanctuary takes some getting used to.''

He had alternately loved and hated the place at different times in his life. But if Damon planned to install her at the house, Alex would limit the amount of time he spent at the estate. His physical awareness of his brother's fiancée was inappropriate.

''Why would I have to get used to it?''

''Forgive me. I was under the impression that you're engaged to my brother.''

Confusion flashed in her eyes. ''But this is your house, not Damon's.''

She didn't know much about the man she was supposedly marrying. ''It's his house, too.'' At least until Alex agreed to sell, something he'd been reluctant to do to the dismay of his family.

The front door crashed open.

Sophie jumped back. She slipped her feet into her shoes and tried to restore order to her clothes. Did she look as guilty as she felt? she wondered. Despite any outward appearance of calm, her insides churned with a multitude of confusing emotions.

Never before had she experienced such an intense reaction to a man. The scent of saddle soap, so utterly masculine and earthy, still lingered. Not only had she literally thrown herself into his arms, she hadn't wanted him to let go. Nice behavior from a supposedly engaged woman!

Damon strode into the library. He came up behind her and slid his hands over her waist. She should have expected him to show a display of affection in his brother's presence, but she couldn't stop herself from twisting away.

"She's a bit shy," Damon explained as he tugged her back to his side.

"Funny," Alex said. "I didn't get that impression."

Sophie felt the blood rush to her cheeks again. As first impressions went, she had certainly given Alex something to think about. She didn't usually dance for an audience.

"Then I guess the two of you had enough time to get acquainted in my absence," Damon said.

"Oh, yes." Alex's half smile sent a surge of heat through her.

She'd certainly had enough time to become acquainted with the hard lines and solid planes of his body. A bit of information she would be wise to forget as soon as possible. She would have to talk to Damon about shortening the length of their stay to a few days. Undoubtedly, she would have made a bad enough impression on his upper-class family by then to achieve his goal.

She should have heeded the warning she'd read in the tarot cards last week. Even her mother had voiced concern via a rare long-distance phone call yesterday. There was no such thing as a *little* white lie. And now, she was in too far to back out.

"So, what do you think?" Damon asked Alex. "Isn't she gorgeous?"

She twisted her fingers together. "He needs glasses."

"There's nothing wrong with his eyesight," Alex said, his gaze never leaving her face.

Damon stroked his finger along her jaw. "Would you like to see your room, babe?"

"Yes, please." Sophie needed to put some distance between herself and Damon's all-too-curious brother. She understood the need for Damon's possessive gestures. After all, he wanted to convince the family they planned to wed. But under Alex's scrutiny, she couldn't repress the sense of guilt that made her want to blurt out the truth.

Did Alex notice her lack of response to her fiancée?

"Which room did Mother have prepared?" Damon asked.

"The guest room in the east wing." Alex arched an eyebrow in amusement. "Unless you want her in your room."

"No!" she said too sharply. She glanced at Damon for help, but he offered none. "I wouldn't insult your mother by sharing a room before we're married."

"Let me get you settled." As Damon took her arm and led her away, she heard Alex's hearty chuckle mocking her.

On the walk to the room she expected Damon to explode with anger at her stiff and unemotional responses. He never did. Instead, he strode up the stairs and down the hall looking very pleased with himself. Only when they entered the bedroom did he say anything at all.

"So, what do you think?"

"The room is beautiful." The polished antique furniture left the faint scent of lemon in the air. The bedspread and drapes, in shades of teal and peacock blue, were the most elegant she had ever seen. She sat on the tapestry-covered window seat and glanced outside. From the second-floor vantage point the woods beyond the stone wall were visible.

"Not the room. What did you think of Alex?"

She turned to face him. "I think he suspects there is something odd about our relationship."

"Besides that?"

"He was polite." Considering she had sent him flying into a wall, he had been downright gracious.

Damon sat on the sleigh bed and tucked a pillow behind his head. "That's all?"

She also happened to think Alex was incredibly sexy in his flannel shirt and jeans, not at all the three-piece-suit type she had been expecting. He had a body to die for, thick eyelashes she would kill for, and warm brown eyes that sent her pulse racing.

And her entire purpose for being here was to make a lousy impression on this man.

Damon waved his hand. "Sophie?"

She blinked and met his amused gaze. "What else do you want? I'm only supposed to have eyes for you, honey."

"He couldn't stop staring at you."

"I was standing right in front of him."

"You were blushing."

She sprung to her feet. "What's going on? Are you trying to set me up with your brother?"

"Of course not," he protested.

"Good. Then we probably won't need to stay the entire week."

"Anxious to leave already?"

"You know us Gypsies. We need to wander."

"We have to stay the week. Really make them worry about our marriage. They'll be so relieved when I dump you that they'll stop interfering in my business."

"How come you get to dump me? Maybe I don't want you."

He grinned and rose to his feet. "You can tell our friends anything you want to save face."

"Get lost."

He reached for the door handle. "By the way...if you should get a case of wanderlust during the night, be careful. Alex has the room next to yours and you share a bathroom."

"What?"

"This wing of the house was originally designed for the master and mistress of the estate." He blew her a kiss and sprinted away.

She dropped down on the bed and sighed. Was Damon trying to play matchmaker? If so, why had he told his family they were engaged? Certainly no brother would intentionally make a play for the other's fiancée. No, Damon must have something else in mind, but she wasn't going to discover what until he was good and ready to tell her.

Alex clicked on the computer and dialed into the office. Although he trusted his manager with the daily running of the company, he wanted to check over the orders for the day—

Nice try, but he wasn't buying his own excuses. He wanted something to take his mind off the sultry beauty who had invaded his home and his thoughts.

He would bet the family business that there was no intimate relationship between Sophie and Damon. She couldn't even pretend to like his touch. What were they up to, and was his stepmother, Elaine, also in on the plan? With six empty bedrooms in the house, why had she chosen to put Sophie in the one next to his, while Elaine and Damon took residence in the opposite wing?

Alex smiled. It wasn't Christmas, although he wouldn't mind unwrapping Sophie under a tree.

He tried to focus on the figures on the computer screen, but he couldn't concentrate. The image of Sophie dancing across the floor as if she were making love to the music, left him with a consuming ache. A kind of hunger he hadn't felt in a long time. If she was brought here to seduce him, she had made one hell of a good start. But to what end?

"I thought you were on vacation." Damon strode into the library and flopped down in a chair.

Alex kept his gaze on the screen. "I didn't close the company down."

"Business good?"

"Yeah." He logged off and leaned back in his seat. "So when's the big day?"

"What big day?"

"Your wedding."

"Oh," Damon mumbled. "Sophie hasn't set a date yet."

Alex laughed. "Smart girl."

"You don't believe I'll go through with it."

"I never gave it a thought either way," he lied smoothly.

"So, what do you think? Does she remind you of anyone?"

Although Alex's first glimpse had brought back old memories, Sophie affected him in a way *no* other woman ever had. On second thought, there hadn't been much of a resemblance at all. Whereas his ex had been a cool, regal beauty, Sophie was the personification of wild passion. "Should she?"

"Don't you think she looks like Marie?"

He feigned bewilderment. "Who?"

"Your ex-fiancée."

"You mean your ex-lover."

"Still holding that against me?" Damon gave him a wounded frown that he pulled off with such practiced ease. "Isn't five years a bit long to be carrying a grudge?"

Alex shrugged as if he couldn't care less. He was grateful he'd found out before the wedding instead of after. Last he heard, his faithless ex was on her third marriage. "You brought her name up, not me."

"You're right. Besides, Sophie is nothing like Marie."

"You mean she's not trying to figure out how much you're worth in alimony before the wedding?"

Damon laughed. "Cheap shot—but true. Marie was a cold bitch." He seemed to have conveniently forgotten his own part in that fiasco.

"Why don't you save yourself the trouble and tell me what this visit is really about?"

"I wanted Sophie to meet my family. Nothing more."

Alex noted that his brother hadn't mentioned any words of love, or even lust. Lord knew, he could sympathize with that. "All right. Play it your way. So, what does she do?"

"She's a graphic artist by trade. Freelance, mostly. But if you're nice to her, you might get her to tell your fortune. She has a real gift for seeing into the future."

"Is that right?" Alex wouldn't mind a peek into the future. Say, one week from today to see what this charade was really about. "I might just ask her."

"She's got real Gypsy blood in her."

A grin pulled at the corners of his mouth. "I don't doubt that. She does make quite an impression." An impression that affected him physically whenever he remembered their encounter.

"So you don't mind if we settle here after the wedding?"

"You'll have to run that past Elaine. Two queens in one castle could make for strained living conditions. Are you sure your little Gypsy will want to live with her mother-in-law?"

"What about you?" Damon's question held a trace of challenge. He was apparently searching for something he could exploit to his benefit.

Alex curled his fingers around a crystal paperweight and tapped it against the oak desk. "It's a big house. I'll adjust when I'm around."

"Of course, I'd prefer to give my wife her own house, but I can't while my money is tied up in this one."

He had wondered how long it would take before Damon brought up the subject. "Your track record with money hasn't been a winning one. You might thank me one day for keeping a roof over your head. Especially if you have a wife to take care of."

"Don't you think it's time you stop trying to protect me from myself? The restaurant was a good investment. I just got in too deep."

Alex refrained from reminding his brother that living way above his means would always get him in too deep. Six years earlier, he had bought out Damon's and Elaine's shares of the company, and neither one had a dime left of their substantial inheritance. Alex would have given in to pressure to sell

the estate, too, only he'd promised his father he
would look out for his stepfamily. Problem was, they
didn't want his help. They wanted unconditional ac-
cess to his money.

"You come talk to me after the wedding and we'll
discuss this again."

Damon slumped forward in the chair. "Why wait?
You always said you'd sell when one of us got married."

"And I will, when you're married. Call it my wedding present to the two of you." Alex was relatively
sure his brother wouldn't be collecting on the gift.
But if he was wrong…? He wasn't ready to contem-
plate the answer.

Two

Sophie slowly opened her eyes. Disoriented, she stared for a few groggy seconds before she realized the white tile ceiling was not her own. After stretching the last of the sleep from her body, she slid her legs over the edge of the bed. How long had she been asleep? A glance out the window gave her the answer. The flaming sun hovered just above the horizon. The long car ride must have wiped her out. It had to be close to eight o'clock.

Why hadn't Damon called her for dinner?

She shed her wrinkled clothes in favor of a pair of black jeans and pale yellow blouse and ran a brush through her hair. She hoped her absence from dinner hadn't been taken as an insult.

As she stepped into the hall, she was surprised by the quiet. No music or sounds of television. Not even the drifting hums of conversation could be heard.

Where was everybody? The clack of her sandals echoed off the high walls. As she descended the stairs,
she repressed the urge to hop on the solid oak ban-
ister and ride to the bottom.

The only signs of life seemed to be coming from
the kitchen. She entered the room to find the butler
and an older woman enjoying a cup of coffee. They
both rose quickly to their feet.

"I'm sorry," Sophie stammered. "I guess I
missed dinner."

"Master Damon said you weren't to be dis-
turbed," the butler said. "I'll have Cook bring a
plate to the dining room for you."

It was bad enough she had rudely slept through
her hosts' evening meal, she wasn't about to have
the staff go out of their way on her behalf. "I'm not
hungry. Where is Damon?"

"He went to the club with his mother for a while.
Master Alexander is around somewhere. Would you
like me to find him?" Such formality seemed more
suited to a feudal system. Did the family always de-
mand such propriety?

"No. I'll just grab an apple or two and take a walk
around."

"As you like, miss."

"Sophie," she corrected.

She swiped two Granny Smiths from the counter
and slipped out the back door. The air, clean and
fresh from the earlier rain, cooled her skin. She
leaned against the stone facade of the house and ate
one of the tart apples to relieve the growling in her
stomach. Her hunger sated, she began exploring the
well-manicured grounds.

Red and white rosebushes ran the outside perimeter of the house. She stroked her fingers over the velvety petals and inhaled the floral scent. Such beauty hidden from the rest of the world, she thought.

The deep purple sky silhouetted a stable and paddock in the distance. She sprinted down the driveway, past the six-car garage and along the worn path to the open door. The wooden building smelled of hay, manure and saddle soap, reminding her of the caravan days of childhood she had spent with her mother. An odd sensation, like a low-voltage shock, ran though her as she stepped inside.

Brass lanterns lit the interior with muted light. The horses shifted nervously at the entrance of a stranger. A chestnut bay poked his nose out of the stall.

"Hello there, fellow." She stroked the hair at his forehead. He snorted and bit the apple out of her hand that rested on top of the gate. "Hey, you big thief. That was my dinner."

He nudged her shoulder.

"Too late, you beggar. I ate the other one."

She raised to her toes and the animal nuzzled its head against her shoulder. "So, what do you do for fun around here? I know. Not much you can do when you're closed in by four walls. I quite understand how you feel."

She scooted down the concrete center aisle to the next stall. "Hey, girl. Don't be shy." She extended her hand and waited for the Appaloosa to come to her. The horse's eyes looked sad and lonely.

"So, what's your problem?" Sophie glanced toward the bay, then back. "Your boyfriend? Just a friend, you say. You have your eye on the Arabian stud?'' She sighed. ''Stay away from the wild ones. They'll break your heart every time.''

The animal's ears perked up and she tapped her hoof several times.

''Feeling restless? Why don't I open all the gates and we'll make a run for it?''

''You'll never clear the wall.''

At the sound of Alex's deep voice, Sophie's breath caught in her throat. She wiped her hands along her jeans and turned to face him. He was leaning against the wall behind her, his arms folded casually over the wide expanse of his chest. A blatantly sexual grin lifted the corners of his mouth.

''Master Alexander. Please except my humble apologies for missing dinner this evening.''

He let out a hearty chuckle. ''An apology's not necessary, and call me Alex. I've been trying to stop William for the past twenty-five years, but he insists on the formal title.''

''Okay. Alex.''

A long silence followed. A few sentences with the man and she had run out of conversation. Her body, on the other hand, had just begun to state its case. Her pulse beat a little faster, her stomach fluttered, and a warm tingling sensation washed over her.

Her conscience warned her to tell him the truth, but she remained silent. The money Damon would donate to the youth center was one reason, but not the only one. This intense and irrational attraction left her confused, an emotion that led to foolish mistakes. She needed the protection her sham engagement afforded her until she figured out how to control the carnal impulses Alex's nearness inspired.

A shove to her back sent her stumbling forward.

She steadied herself by grabbing onto Alex's shoulders. His hands came up to encircle her waist.

"What the heck…" She glanced back to see the Appaloosa shaking her head.

"Now, now, Delilah. She's Damon's woman. No matchmaking."

"Is that what she's doing?" The animal had good aim—and even better instincts, Sophie decided.

She held on to Alex longer than necessary. While her mind willed her to step back to regain her senses, her body begged her to stay put, surrounded by warmth, protected by strength.

Reason prevailed and she wriggled out of his arms. "Sorry."

"So, you want to make a break from this place already?" He reached into his vest pocket for a sugar cube and offered it to Delilah.

Sophie stood next to him and scratched the animal behind the ear. "I was just making conversation with them."

"Do you ride?"

"Yes."

"English or Western?"

"Bareback, mostly."

"Really?" He couldn't keep the surprise from his voice.

"Really."

"You're welcome to ride while you're here."

"I'd like to." Sophie smiled at him and Alex was stunned by the way his body reacted to the genuine excitement he saw in her flushed face. "Maybe I'll get Damon to take me."

The mention of his brother deflated some of the

air from his ego. "He doesn't ride. But don't let that stop you."

"I wouldn't."

Alex swallowed a chuckle. He would guess the lady did as she pleased. Not for the first time, he wondered why she had chosen to involve herself with Damon. "I wonder if my brother knows what he's gotten himself into."

"He should. I've known him for four years. We have an understanding."

He arched his eyebrow. "What kind of understanding?"

"Obviously not the kind you're thinking of." She rolled her eyes. "We have different interests that we pursue separately."

"That would explain why he's at the country club playing racquetball while you're here trying to incite a rebellion among my horses."

Her soft exhale of laughter caressed his cheek. "I couldn't interest them. They must like living with walls."

"Which, I gather, you don't?"

"I don't have to, do I?"

"My brother seems to think you're going to settle here after the wedding." Her guilty expression was telling. He suspected that she and Damon hadn't synchronized their stories.

She shrugged and raked a handful of curls from her face. "Actually, we didn't discuss it. We haven't had time to figure out our future yet."

Nice recovery. She wouldn't have to worry now if they contradicted each other. The woman was bright. He would have an easier time tripping up Damon. Something shady was going on and Alex meant to find out what before his conniving brother did any damage. Any more damage, he mentally corrected.

"Come on. I'll take you up to the house so you can get something to eat. Samson ate your apple."

"Samson and Delilah. That's cute. What are the other two called?"

"Windancer," he said, pointing to a jet-black Arabian. "And…Elvis."

"Elvis," she cried out, sending a sympathetic smile to the gelding. "Oh, the indignity of it all. No wonder he's so shy." Dramatic sighs and theatrical gestures punctuated her words.

"He was already named when I got him."

"Poor thing." She locked her fingers together behind her back and walked alongside Alex to the house. Darkness had descended and a starry landscape sparkled above.

"So, how did you and Damon meet?" he asked to break the silence.

"I worked for him at the restaurant while I was going to school. We remained good friends after he sold the place."

Sold the place. Is that what Damon had told her? Alex opened the back door and waited for her to enter. "Have a seat. I'll get you something—"

"No need."

"Cook already made the plate. I'm just going to stick it in the microwave."

"Yum. Radioactive food," she muttered, and lowered herself into a chair at the drop-leaf table.

Alex put the covered plate in the oven and thanks to modern technology, served her a hot meal in mere minutes. After pouring two glasses of wine, he joined her at the table. "Go ahead. Eat."

Sophie nodded her thanks and enthusiastically dug in. She polished off the veal and sautéed potatoes with a fervor that nearly rivaled her dancing. In his experience, most women became falsely modest when eating in front of a man. Sophie became down-right sexy. Did she devote the same passion to every aspect of her life?

Alex swallowed a grunt. Thoughts like that would land him in trouble. "Damon tells me you have Gypsy blood."

She put down her fork and knife. "Yes. And we're notorious thieves, so you better hide the family silver."

He thought perhaps he had insulted her, but when she glanced up, her eyes shone with mischievous humor. "I'm not worried. So, will you look into your crystal ball and tell me my future?"

"I don't use a crystal ball, and I can't see the future. But I sometimes get strong impressions about people."

He leaned closer until his shoulder brushed hers. "What about me?"

She smiled and took his hand. Her sensual touch, as she stroked her thumb over his palm and wrist, sent his pulse racing. She inched closer until her leg made contact with his. Her delicate eyebrow raised in a perplexed arch. "I'm getting something."

"What?"

During the long pause, she stared at him. She ran her tongue nervously over her full lips, leaving a glistening shine. He swallowed hard. She continued to caress his calloused flesh, sending jolting electrodes through his entire being. He shifted in the wooden chair to relieve the tightening in his groin.

Suddenly she dropped his hand, looking startled and gasping for breath. Her round emerald eyes, hypnotic, exotic and blatantly erotic, held him spellbound.

"What's wrong?" he asked.

"I'm getting a really strong impression…" She paused, and inhaled deeply. Her gaze locked with his. "That you're patronizing me."

He blinked slowly and let out a groan. Perhaps he had been humoring her, but she had paid him back with interest. She'd had him so mesmerized, she could have told him aliens were attacking and he would have believed her.

"All right. Let's talk about something else."

She lifted her wineglass toward him in a salute, then took a sip. "Should we play twenty questions?"

"How else will I get to know my future sister-in-law?"

"When do we get to the part about how I'm totally wrong for Damon?"

"I don't believe that."

"You don't?"

He believed Damon was wrong for *her*. Damon hadn't grown up yet. And Alex wouldn't be the least bit surprised if his brother had used his charm to convince Sophie to go through with the marriage just to get him to sell the house.

"I'm looking forward to your wedding." He managed to say the words without gagging. "When are you going to set a date?"

Absently, she chewed her bottom lip and toyed with the gold chain around her neck. "Ah…um…"

"In this millennium or the next?"

"I'm only twenty-six. My biological clock isn't

ticking away. Besides, I haven't even met his mother yet. She might want some input on the time and place.''

Alex tipped his head. ''I'm sure Elaine will have something to say.''

''Is that a warning?''

''No.'' He took a gulp of his wine.

''Damon said she's anxious for grandchildren.''

Alex nearly choked. He slapped his hand to his chest. ''Excuse me. Swallowed wrong.''

Elaine was about as anxious to be a grandmother as she was to get another wrinkle on her surgically lifted face. She didn't even like to admit to having a thirty-year-old son.

Sophie collected her dishes from the table and loaded them into the dishwasher. ''Thanks for dinner. I guess Damon and his mom will be late. I'm going to turn in.''

Alex rose and walked her to the staircase. Since she had spent most of the afternoon sleeping, he figured she wanted to avoid him. Apparently his comments and questions were in contrast to what Damon had told her. Why would his brother lie to his fiancée? Or, more important, to his accomplice?

''Good night,'' she called over her shoulder as she ascended the stairs.

Once she reached the top landing, Sophie darted down the hall to her room. Damn Damon and the awkward position he had put her in! She let out a groan. *Face it, Sophie. You're the one who's pretending to be somebody you're not.*

Perhaps a look into the cards would help, she decided, as she reached for the silk pouch on the dresser. She untied the ribbon and removed her tarot cards. Her mother had presented her with the deck on her eighteenth birthday. A piece of her past to guide her future. While she absently shuffled, she tried to formulate a question in her mind.

Do I have reason to worry about my actions?

She sat cross-legged on the bed and dealt out ten cards in a semicircle. Each of the first nine cards represented the influence going on around her and the last, her answer. She flipped over the first one and let out a nervous laugh. The Four of Wands. An interlude with a man. She didn't need the tarot to tell her that. What kind of interlude? Next, she turned the Ten of Cups, upside down, which symbolized a betrayal. Damon? Or Alex? The cards weren't clear.

The Two of Wands, meant to indicate her fears, pointed to the *lord of the manor.* A chill ran along her spine. Alex was definitely at the root of her fears, but she didn't know why. Having a serious case of the hots for a man wasn't lethal as long as she kept her head clear.

The rest of the reading wasn't any more encouraging than the beginning. The cards predicted an upheaval in her entire way of life. The sooner she left The Sanctuary, the better.

A sharp knock on her door gave Sophie a start. She scooped the deck back into a neat pile. "It's open," she called out.

Damon sauntered inside. "Hey, Soph, you finally rose from the dead."

She shot him an icy glare. "With no help from you. Why didn't you wake me for dinner?"

He eyed her as if she was crazy. "I've called you in the morning. I know what you're like when you wake up."

"Okay. That's fair," she grumbled. "So, did you speak with your mother?"

He leaned against the rolltop desk and grinned. "She's not happy. Kept trying to introduce me to suitable girls from the club, but I told her it was you or no one."

"Good." She slipped off the bed and took a seat by the window. "Because your brother doesn't seem all that opposed to this *marriage.*"

"Stepbrother," Damon corrected.

"Funny. Alex never makes that distinction."

"He might say he doesn't care, but give him a few days. He'll change his tune. He won't be able to resist the opportunity to blow something he thinks I want."

She raised her head. "And you plan to convince him you couldn't live without me by leaving me alone and going off to the club on your first night here?"

"Are you mad at me? I thought you hated places like that."

"I do. And I'm not mad. I'm just questioning your methods. He already suspects something's not right."

"Even better. He'll think you're after my money."

"Oh, great." she let out on a frustrated exhale of breath. "Being unorthodox isn't enough. I have to be a social-climbing weirdo. I thought I wouldn't mind, but I don't like lying." At least, not to Alex.

"Let me ease your conscience." He dropped to one knee. "Sophie Anders, will you marry me? There, I proposed. Now you're not lying."

"And you'd bolt like lightning if I said yes."

He chuckled. "After I stopped laughing. You want

to get married even less than I do. That's one of the main reasons I asked you to help me.''

''That, and I'm the strangest person you know.''

''True.'' He stood up and brushed the wrinkles from his designer jeans. ''Who else would spend her vacation traveling with a carnival?''

''I was visiting my mother,'' she corrected with a defiant lift of her chin.

''And reading tarot cards on the side,'' he reminded her.

She waved an accusing finger at him. ''It paid better than you did.''

''I give up.'' He paced around the room. ''So, what did you do while I was out?''

''Visited the stables.''

''Passed the time with Alex, huh?''

She drew her brows together. ''Why would you say that?''

''He's always with those horses when he's home. I'm surprised he doesn't sleep in a stall.'' Damon grimaced in distaste. ''So, what did you talk about?''

''Check your ego. We talked more about the horses than we did about you.'' She nestled herself into the window seat and gazed at the glittering sky. At night, when she couldn't see the wall, the place didn't seem so bad. ''Alex said I was welcome to ride while I was here.''

''Good. Then I don't feel so bad that I signed up for a racquetball tournament at the club for the next couple of days.''

''You wouldn't have felt bad anyway.''

''You're right.'' He gave her a boyish grin, then saluted as he left the room. She didn't return the smile.

Strange. The very qualities she had once admired in Damon weren't quite so endearing anymore. He could be funny, charming—the life of any party. As long as he got what he wanted and didn't have to give of himself in return. More unsettling was the realization that she could easily become like him if she continued with her current life-style.

Three

――――――

Sophie hovered just outside the dining room door. The aroma of cinnamon hung in the air. She had been awake for nearly three hours, waiting for Damon and his mother to get up. She understood that the family was on vacation, but sleeping in until almost noon blew the best part of the day. Taking a deep breath for courage, she entered the room. The conversation came to an abrupt end.

Damon smiled and rose. "Mother, this is Sophie."

Sophie glanced at Elaine Sinclair. Not a platinum hair was out of place. Her makeup, applied to perfection, and her tailored suit gave the impression of a much younger woman than Sophie had expected. Where was the matronly housewife who longed for grandchildren that Damon had described?

"It's a pleasure to meet you." Sophie offered her hand to the older woman.

"I'm sure." Elaine barely made contact before withdrawing her fingers. She gave a disinterested glance at Sophie's appearance.

Her outfit—a pair of denim shorts, a white halter top and a sweatshirt tied around her waist—had seemed appropriate vacation wear when she'd dressed. Who knew that breakfast attire was formal at The Sanctuary? Even Damon had worn a silk shirt and tie. Tucking her bare feet beneath her, she settled into a Windsor chair next to Damon. The maid served a cup of tea and left a small basket of croissants in front of her plate. She picked off the edge of the flaky bread and popped it in her mouth.

"Where are your people from?" Elaine asked casually, but there was nothing casual about the icy glare she shot Sophie.

Sophie brushed the hair off her shoulder. "Originally or currently?"

"Currently."

"My mother is somewhere around Kansas right now. She's...on tour."

"An actress?" Elaine grumbled with obvious distaste.

"No. A fortune-teller with the Vitabel Traveling Carnival."

"And your father?"

Sophie looked to Damon for assistance. Instead of helping, he leaned back in his seat and sipped his espresso. He seemed to enjoy his mother's grilling. "I never met my father."

"I see. And do you travel with the circus, too?"

"Carnival," Sophie corrected. "And I did move with my mother when I was a child, until the courts said she had to enroll me in school. Then we moved to New York with my grandmother.''

''A sideshow performer, too, I presume?''

Sophie had never felt embarrassed about her family and Elaine Sinclair's snobbish airs wouldn't change that.

''What is this? The Spanish Inquisition?'' The familiar deep voice sent a tingle along her spine.

Elaine tensed as Alex strode into the room. ''Alex, dear. I thought you were in the stables.''

''I came in for lunch, but apparently you're still on breakfast.'' Dressed all in black, he radiated pure masculine sexuality. ''Good morning, Sophie. Damon.''

Sophie waved. ''How's Elvis this morning?''

He chuckled. ''Going through an identity crisis. You shouldn't have laughed at his name. He's got some attitude today.''

''I'll talk to him.''

''Thanks, but you've done enough.''

She grinned sheepishly and took a sip of tea. She credited the warmth spreading through her to the hot liquid rather than Alex's smile.

Elaine drummed her fingernails against the table. ''What time are we leaving for the club, Damon?''

''About an hour.'' He cupped his fingers possessively over Sophie's arm. ''You coming, honey?''

She shook her head. ''Only if you tranquilize me first.''

''A few hours with the horses will put you to sleep.''

''Ten minutes of watching you prance around a racquetball court will do it, too,'' she teased back, wrinkling her nose.

"She loves me," Damon announced with a laugh. "Come on, babe, I need to talk to you before I leave."

Sophie was happy to comply. She needed to get out of the cross fire and regroup. Why had Damon allowed his brother to come to her defense rather than standing up for her himself? Did he really think his mother would be fooled by their supposed engagement when he showed her no more affection and concern than he would show the butler? Digging her fingernails into the arm he offered her, she followed Damon out of the room.

Alex lowered his head and watched a delicate pair of bare feet with red toenails pass by him. He struggled against the urge to examine the rest of Sophie's body as she left the room. The more often he saw her, the harder he had to fight the attraction he felt. Listening to his stepmother question Sophie in her judgmental and demeaning way had brought out his protective instinct. Seeing Sophie, head held high and unruffled by the verbal snipes, he realized she neither wanted nor needed his help.

Elaine pushed back her plate and folded her linen napkin. "Well?"

Alex poured a mug of coffee and grabbed a piece of toast. "Well, what?"

"You can't possibly mean to let Damon marry that woman."

"Since when have I had any influence with him?"

"She's totally inappropriate."

He leaned against the wall. "I think she's perfect for him." Despite his own feelings he managed to keep a straight face. He didn't want Sophie for a sister-in-law. He just plain wanted her. And he instinctively knew that his brother had known he would.

Elaine's jaw sagged. "What?"

"Sure. One of those country-club debutantes would bore him inside a week and bankrupt what little he has left in a month."

"And you think Gypsy Woman isn't after his money?"

"If that's the case, she'll be gone as soon as she realizes he doesn't have any."

"Alex, are you telling me you won't do anything about this engagement?"

"What do you want me to do?"

"You'll be here. Spend some time with her. See what she's up to."

He was more interested in what his family was up to. Damon couldn't bother sticking around to entertain his own fiancée. Elaine might as well have asked Alex to seduce Sophie. Why?

Why not? The thought brought a smile to his lips.

"Alex, he'll ruin his life and marry her just to get you to sell the house. Have you thought about that?"

"Yes. And I'm sure he has, too." He grabbed another slice of toast on his way out.

How far was his family willing to go in their endeavors to get him to sell the estate? This wouldn't be the first time Damon had enlisted the aid of a beautiful woman in his quest. However, if this was another scam, he'd make damn sure it was the last one.

Sophie entered the stall slowly with her hand held out. "Come on, Elvis. I'll call you the King if you come out. No saddle. I promise.'' She coaxed the horse forward and slipped the bridle over his head. ''That's not so bad.''

She walked him out of the stable. After tossing her backpack on her shoulder, she used the paddock fence as a leg up onto Elvis's broad back. A click of her tongue and pressure from her legs started the animal moving, but he stopped short a moment later when Alex drew up alongside.

''Where are you going?'' His biceps rippled as he stroked the horse's head. Streaks of gold highlighted his tawny brown hair.

''The King and I are going for a stroll. Is that all right?''

''I said you were welcome to ride, but wouldn't you rather I went with you until you know your way around?''

She waved her hand at the panoramic view before her. ''It's hard to get lost in a fortress.''

''I thought you might want to explore beyond the wall.''

Although she would be wise to keep her distance from Alex, the temptation to go AWOL was more than she could refuse. ''If it's not too much trouble.''

''I'm going anyway,'' he said with an indifferent shrug of his shoulders.

She let out an exaggerated sigh. Despite his nonchalant air, she wondered if he had already decided to go to keep an eye on her. ''Well, gee, control your enthusiasm.''

''This is as excited as I get about anything.''

She bit her lower lip to prevent a full-blown laugh from erupting. Was that ever a challenge, her overactive hormones wanted to answer. What would it take to make him lose control?

Shaking her head, she exhaled slowly. She would never know. Not while he believed her to be involved with his brother. And if he learned the truth? He would probably trust her even less.

Alex grabbed a saddle and tack. "Give me five minutes."

She nodded and urged Elvis toward the driveway.

Alex joined her moments later. Sitting astride Windancer like a legendary Western outlaw, he was the sexiest man she'd ever seen. A comfortable silence settled between them as they rode side by side toward the main entrance. The farther they got from the house, the lighter she felt. Was it the estate that made her feel so oppressed—or her own guilt?

Once they cleared the gate, Sophie looked back over her shoulder at the high wall with cameras mounted on each side.

"My father was paranoid about security," Alex said.

"Considering your past, it's understandable." She cursed the words the second she uttered them.

He sat ramrod straight in the saddle. His jaw clenched and his eyes flashed with anger. "Damon told you."

She bowed her head. "Yes. And he expressly told me not to say anything. But, as usual, my mouth was engaged before my brain was in gear."

"A frequent occurrence with you, I've noticed." He stared at her for a long moment, then smiled, revealing two beautiful dimples. "I prefer unguarded honesty to a well-rehearsed lie."

Her stomach muscles tightened. No matter how

quickly he'd recovered, she had still touched on a raw nerve. "I'm sorry."

"It's not a state secret. You can pick up an old newspaper and find stories about the incident."

"I don't dig into other people's pasts. Mine isn't a Norman Rockwell portrait."

"As long as Damon doesn't mind…"

She pretended not to hear. Her relationship with Damon was not a subject she wished to discuss. Alex already had his doubts. Why add to his suspicions by proving how little she knew about her fiancé?

"Which way?" she asked.

He looked as if he wanted to ask her something, then shook his head. "To the right."

Alex led the way along the tree-lined road. The clack of the horses' shoes against the asphalt drummed a calypso beat. Once they cleared the western wall, Sophie saw the wooded area with well-worn paths. A rainbow at the end of a storm, she thought. She allowed Elvis to wander through the maze of foliage in any direction he chose.

Beads of perspiration rolled down her back. Another muggy July day was underway. She took an elastic band from her shorts' pocket and loosely tied back her hair, as beams of sunlight filtered through the tall oaks and pine trees.

She was intensely aware of Alex's presence, his constant gaze fixed on her. She had even come to accept the erotic sensations that his nearness inspired. Getting a clear impression of him, however, was virtually impossible. Had her strong sexual awareness of him left her unable to read the man beneath the guarded mask?

"Where are we?" she asked.

"We're still on our property. The boundary is the stream up ahead."

As they approached the rolling brook, Sophie brought her horse to a halt and slipped off his back. "Do you mind?"

She glanced up at Alex atop his jet-black Arabian. A breath caught in her throat. When Damon had promised her an exciting vacation in beautiful New England, he hadn't warned her just what kind of excitement she would be in for.

"We can stop here for a while." He dismounted, a graceful movement that revealed the muscles of his well-toned body.

She sighed longingly.

"Did you say something?" he asked.

"No."

"Oh. I thought you did." A lopsided grin tugged at his mouth. Had he read her mind?

He took the reins of both animals and tied them to a tree. Sophie settled herself on a rock, dangling her toes into the cold water. From her backpack, she took a sketch pad and charcoal. She ran a gaze over the landscape.

Alex sat with his back to the trunk of a big, old maple tree. He extended one leg straight out and bent the other, resting his arm across his knee. Now that was a sight she wanted to capture, Sophie thought. Pure sex appeal in one gorgeous package.

"You're a graphic artist?" he asked.

She divided her gaze between Alex and the sketch pad. "Yes."

"Get a lot of work?"

"It pays the bills. I just finished a big project and I have a few smaller ones lined up when I get back."

"I could use a new catalog."

Was he serious or merely making conversation? It occurred to her that she had no idea how Alex earned a living. "Oh yeah, for what?"

"A product catalog and new price lists for the coming year. What do you suggest I do to jazz up a catalog for cardboard cartons?"

She glanced up from her drawing. "Aside from having them photographed next to a model in a skimpy bathing suit?"

"I never tried that. Would you be the model?"

She crinkled her nose in distaste. "Are the boxes made of recycled paper?"

"As a matter of fact, yes. Why? Are you a spy for Greenpeace?"

"I was thinking more along the lines of playing the ecology angle up in the catalog, but I guess you were patronizing me again rather than seriously asking my opinion."

He frowned. "I was serious about a catalog. Where's your sense of humor?"

Buried under a mountain of bewilderment, she thought. Why had she sought approval like some awestruck adolescent? And why had she felt hurt when she thought she had failed? She needed to get a grip before she did something stupid. In her twenty-six years she had never lost her head over any man. She couldn't afford to start now.

"Is there a big market for cardboard cartons?"

"Every company ships in boxes. It's not as exciting as owning a restaurant, but it's a hell of a lot more stable."

"I never understood why Damon sold the restaurant. I guess he didn't like having a partner. But he's got his eye on a club in the Village.''

''Is that right?'' Alex lowered his head and closed his eyes. Now he knew why Damon wanted to get his hands on cash.

He inhaled the fresh country air and let the gentle roll of the water relax him. For the moment, he could almost forget that less than three feet away sat a woman who might be setting him up. But he couldn't forget the woman. That white slip of a shirt she wore revealed the swells of her breasts every time she leaned forward. Committed to memory were those long dancer's legs and the way she had used her strong thighs to control Elvis over the uneven ground.

So much for alleviating the tension. If his body was wound any tighter, he would bust his jeans. Occasionally he opened one eye, but Sophie was too engrossed in her work to notice. Her expression, a combination of confusion and determination, left him wondering what was on her mind.

''Alex?'' The sound of her husky voice caressed his ear. He remained silent just to hear her call his name again. Leaves rustled as she walked toward him. ''Are you asleep?'' she whispered.

Although he knew he should answer, he waited, curious to see what she had in mind. Her shadow moved across him. She stepped around the tree. The scratch of a zipper along metal runners was followed by the thump of her shorts hitting the ground. Was she planning to run naked through the forest?

Only when he heard her splashing in the water did he dare to move. To his relief and disappointment, she had only stripped down to her satiny undergarments. The peach-colored triangles of material left little to the imagination. Her body was a perfect combination of rounded curves and sleek lines.

Feeling the need for a cold dousing himself, he dragged his gaze away. While she played in the shallow stream, he reached for the sketch pad on the rock and thumbed through the pages.

Sophie had quite a talent for portraits, catching the hope of the future in a child's smile or the pain of life in an old woman's tearstained face. More than pictures, she seemed to capture the souls of her subjects. Perhaps she had been serious when she said she got strong impressions about people.

The last portrait was of him. He was surprised by the likeness, but more by how she viewed him. Arrogance with a hint of anger filled his eyes. His mouth was curved upward in a sardonic smile. And he thought he hid his emotions well.

He glanced back to the stream. She was resting on her elbows, her back arched to dangle her hair in the water. He should feel guilty for his voyeuristic indulgence, but that wasn't the particular emotion the sight invoked. Pure lust came to mind.

When she finally rose, he returned to his position behind the tree. Dressing while wet must have been difficult because she let out several frustrated groans as she tried to twist into her clothes.

"Have a nice dip?" he asked when she strode by him.

She let out a gasp and fumbled with her zipper. "How long have you been awake?"

"I was never asleep."

Her cheeks took on a healthy blush. "Why didn't you answer me?"

"Would you have taken a dip?"

She smoothed her sweatshirt over her shorts. "Of course not."

"I didn't want to deprive you of the obvious pleasure."

"You're such a gentleman," she sniped.

He laughed. "If I were a gentleman, I wouldn't have watched. But don't worry. Your secret is safe with me."

"That makes me feel better." Her narrowed eyes glared threateningly at him. She snatched her pad from his hands. "Did you go through my backpack, too?"

"No."

"It's nice to know that some things are sacred." Leaning against the rock, she brushed her feet and slipped on her sneakers. When she tied the last lace, she sprinted over to the horses.

Alex followed, clamping his hands over her shoulders before she could pull herself up onto Elvis. Damp strands of her hair brushed against his arm as she turned to face him.

"Don't bother to apologize," she said.

"I wasn't going to. You were the one playing Lady Godiva in the stream."

Her eyes ignited with anger. She was absolutely magnificent in her fury. "I was just as covered as if I had been wearing a bathing suit."

"I know. So why are you mad?"

"I'm not," she huffed.

He chuckled. "Then there's no need for us to leave."

Four

————

Sophie expelled a groan. She wasn't mad. She was embarrassed and...aroused. Staring at Alex for a half hour, memorizing and duplicating every angle and curve had left her in an overheated state. She had gone into the water to cool off. Even now, his earthy scent was causing a heat wave in her chilled body. These erratic and erotic impulses would have to stop!

He slid his hand along her arm, then caught hold of her wrist as she started to back away. "I want to ask you something."

She drew in a deep breath and exhaled slowly. "You can ask, but I don't guarantee I'll answer."

"Why is Damon throwing us together?"

She had virtually forgotten about her *beloved fiancé* and her counterfeit engagement. Understandable, when her intended's stepbrother could make her forget her own name with a glance.

"You offered to come with me. That had nothing to do with him. He did invite me to go to the club." She felt like a hypocrite defending Damon when Alex was right.

"And he knew you'd decline. He could have taken you somewhere else today."

"He signed up for a racquetball tournament at the club."

He started to say something, then paused and shook his head. His thumb absently stroked her palm, following the groove formed by her heart line. She felt the effects in far more intimate parts of her body.

"Why bother getting married if you plan to live separate lives?"

His question cooled her as effectively as a cold shower. She gave a hard tug to free her hand and stepped back, bumping into Elvis. Turning to the animal as a much needed distraction, she untied the reins from the tree. "Getting married doesn't mean we have to become Siamese twins."

"It doesn't mean you should live in different time zones, either. Marriage is a compromise."

"If you're such an expert, why haven't you compromised yourself yet?"

He laughed. "Point taken."

"Can you give me a leg up, please?"

He gripped his fingers over her calf and lifted her easily onto Elvis. His hand remained on her leg even after she settled on the horse. "Do you know the way back?"

"Yes."

"Good. I want to take Windancer for a run."

She lifted an eyebrow. "Elvis only strolls?"

"You don't have a saddle."

"You worry about keeping your own backside off the ground and I'll worry about mine." She gathered up the reins and turned Elvis in the direction of the path. Before Alex had a chance to mount, she commanded the horse to a gallop.

Moments later, Alex emerged from the woods and onto the main road directly behind Sophie. Although Windancer could easily overtake the older gelding, he pulled back on the reins. She had told him to watch his own rear end, but he preferred watching hers.

Wind lifted the dark waves of her silky hair. Unlike the uptight, country-club women he was used to, Sophie was uninhibited and perhaps a little reckless as well. The way she rose and fell with the horse's movement brought to mind a more erotic image of making love to her. The saddle beneath him became damned uncomfortable. He loosened the reins and pushed Windancer to race through the gates ahead of Elvis.

"Show-off," she yelled to him.

He raised his hand in a backward wave. When he reached the stable, he jumped from the horse and waited for Sophie to catch up.

A few moments later, she slipped off of Elvis and stroked his neck. "Don't you let it bother you. If we named him Elvis and made him a gelding, he wouldn't be so uppity either." She placed a gentle kiss on the animal's forehead.

"Are you referring to Windancer?"

"No. You."

"Ouch." He lifted the saddle from his mount and put it away.

"Where's the brush?"

"Let them walk it off in the paddock first. I'll take care of them later."

"I'll help."

"Okay. Why don't you bring out Samson and Delilah? Their stalls need to be mucked out."

She crinkled her adorable nose at him. "Gee, thanks. Don't you have help to take care of that?"

"Yeah. But he has the week off while I'm here."

"You don't live here all the time?"

"No. I live outside of Stamford. Didn't Damon tell you?"

She shook her head and glanced at the floor. "He might have said something, but it didn't click at the time."

Placing his thumb under her chin, he tilted her head back. "Why don't you admit it? He never mentioned me until an hour before you arrived here."

"A week," she corrected, but with a trace of apology in her voice. Sadness sparked in the depths of her eyes.

"Forget it. Damon and I have a long history."

She closed her fingers over his forearm. "Despite your relationship with your brother, I hope we can be friends."

Friends? He wanted a hell of a lot more than that from her. "I don't think so."

She looked wounded. "Why?"

"Because I spend too much time thinking about how I want to do this." He lowered his head, muffling her gasp of surprise under the pressure of his mouth. His tongue pushed open her tightly pursed lips, sweeping inside and tasting what he had hungered for all day.

This wasn't one of his brighter ideas, but it felt

better than anything he'd done in a long time. Burying his fingers in her soft mane of curls, he held her to him. Her eyelashes fluttered closed. A sigh became a moan and she surrendered to the moment.

But Sophie didn't play the submissive role for long. In a short time she became the aggressor. She pressed her palms against his chest, moving him back until he came up against a hard wall. Hot kisses covered his face, his neck, his throat. Did she know what she was doing? There was no hesitation in the hands that roamed over his back and shoulders. Her touch was electrifying, jolting to life a part of him he'd thought long dead.

Cupping his fingers over her firm round bottom, he settled her between his thighs. They fit together perfectly, like two halves of a matched set. She brushed her hips across him, smiling when she felt his body shudder in response.

Damn. He wanted to take her right there in the stable, and she didn't act as if she was about to stop him. On the contrary, she already had her hands on his belt buckle as if her desires mirrored his own. "Still think we can be friends, Sophie?"

Her passion-filled gaze locked on him and she froze. "No." Her barely whispered answer spoke volumes. Regret certainly, but a distinct hint of fear, too. She wriggled out of his arms. "Sorry."

"Sorry? That's it?" How could she respond to him with unbridled desire while claiming to be engaged to another man? What had Damon promised her and, more important, what had he asked her to do?

"Thank you?" she amended with obvious sarcasm.

Alex glared coldly.

She pushed back a handful of ringlets from her face and groaned. "What do you want me to say?"

"How about the truth?"

She slipped her hands into her pockets with a rueful shrug and started to walk away. "I'm not sure I know what it is anymore."

"Sophie, wait." She ignored his plea and sprinted to the house without looking back.

He leaned against the wall and exhaled slowly. His body was still rock hard and throbbing with desire. She was either an incredible actress or a very conflicted woman. He aimed to find out which before he ended up in just the kind of trouble he'd sworn to avoid.

Sophie felt a shadow fall across her face. She had parked herself on the backyard patio rather than chance running into Alex. Baking in the summer sun had done little to relieve her heated embarrassment. Bracing her hands on the arms of the redwood lounger, she raised one eye. She wasn't sure if she was relieved or furious to find Damon towering over her.

"How did you spend your day?" he asked.

She pulled her sunglasses from the top of her head and settled them on the bridge of her nose. "I went riding with Alex."

Damon fell into a chair with a grunt. "And did he bore you to death with stories of what a womanizing louse I am?"

"He never said a bad word about you. You, on the other hand, always have something to say about him and I'm beginning to wonder how much is truth and how much is horse…manure.''

His eyes rounded in surprise. "Are you upset about something?"

She sucked in a large gulp of air, hoping to retain the tentative hold she had on her temper. "Yeah, and I want some straight answers or I'm on the next bus to New York."

"What do you want to know?"

"I'm not here for the sole purpose of getting your family off your case about marriage, am I?"

He leaned forward, resting his elbows on his knees. "What did Alex tell you?"

"Nothing." He didn't have to. His questions had left her with too few answers.

"Have you ever been in love, Sophie?"

Damon's query took her by surprise. "No."

"Well, I was once. Crazy in love. Hard to believe, but true." His expression was solemn, reflecting all the pain of love lost.

"What does that have to do with why I'm here?"

"The woman was Alex's ex-fiancée. She broke off with him a week before the wedding. Of course, when she found out most of the Sinclair money went to Alex, she dumped me, too, but by then the damage was done. I've been paying for that mistake for almost five years."

She slid to the edge of the cushioned recliner. She wasn't sure she liked where the story was going. "Where do I fit into this?"

"You know, you're like his Arabian horse. A little wild, untamed."

"Why, thank you," she muttered dryly. "If that's supposed to be a compliment, it didn't work for me."

"I knew he'd find you irresistible and that he would make it his personal mission to rescue you from a rot like me. If he thinks he has 'broken us up,' then the score will be even."

She sprung to her feet. "Are you out of your mind?"

"If you can't see that he's interested, then you're not as bright as I thought."

"That's not the point. You lied to me." In the four years she had known Damon, she had been aware that he was self-centered and self-indulgent where women were concerned. But she'd overlooked his faults because she had considered him a true and honest friend, there for her when she'd needed him. They had always been straight with each other. At least she'd thought they had.

"You wouldn't have come."

"You're damn right. This is beyond a doubt the most rotten thing you've ever done."

"I brought two people together who have a lot of common interests."

"By lying to both of us. Besides, I'm not looking for a man in my life."

"I didn't expect you'd end up married to each other." He expelled a deep groan. "Are you telling me that if you had met Alex on your own, you wouldn't have gone out with him?"

She balled her fingers into tight fists. "This is different. He thinks we're involved. And I don't like being used as a pawn between the two of you."

His expression changed to one of genuine concern. "I never meant to hurt you. But, face it, it's not as if you let your emotions get involved in your intimate relationships. I figured you and Alex would have some fun. I'd play the wounded but forgiving brother, and we wouldn't have this wall between us any longer.''

Was she really as cold-blooded as he made her sound? Thinking back, she had never let a man close enough to hurt her, but she had never intentionally hurt anyone either. ''And what makes you think I'm interested in an affair with your brother?''

He gave her a smile that spoke volumes yet said nothing at all. ''I'm sure it would help if he were a jerk, but as I've often heard you lament, any man is capable of becoming a jerk.''

''And you've proved it with this one, Damon. I will not make a play for your brother so you can score some kind of brownie points with him.''

''I don't expect you to. If you feel uncomfortable, then forget the whole thing. I don't want this to ruin our friendship. Just relax and enjoy your vacation. No pressure.''

Her first thought was to pack her bags and hightail it out of town before sundown. Given the past history between the brothers, she couldn't help wonder why Alex had kissed her earlier. Was he only interested in getting even with Damon? Pain settled over her chest. She was developing feelings for Alex.

She had racked herself with guilt about lying for Damon while feeling attracted to Alex. Now she felt betrayed by both men.

''Come on, Soph. Stay a few more days.''

''Fine. I'll stay,'' she found herself saying, but she had no idea why. ''But I'm not going to lie anymore. As far as I'm concerned, I'm here as your friend, nothing more.''

Damon nodded and rose to his feet. He looked

genuinely contrite. One lie in the four years she had know him could be forgiven. Or was this only the first time she had ever caught him?

She poked a finger into his shoulder and met his apologetic gaze with an icy glare. "But if you ever lie to me again, our friendship will be history along with me."

He grabbed her hand and kissed the back of it. "You're the greatest."

"Sure." She shrugged and walked with him back to the house. "Your own brother's fiancée?" she muttered.

He hooked his arm through hers. "What can I say? When I screw up, I do it royally."

"You certainly do."

While she was flaming mad that he'd involved her in his scheme in any way, she couldn't fault him for trying to make amends with his brother—no matter how misguided his plan.

Alex walked through the silent stables, checking all the gates. He had finished feeding the horses over an hour ago but he was in no hurry to return to the house. Usually he preferred his own company, but thoughts of Sophie kept invading his solitude. Since seeing her earlier, walking across the lawn arm in arm with Damon, he had avoided her.

Windancer nudged his shoulder. "Women are nothing but trouble."

Delilah snorted and he could have sworn she was answering his heartfelt complaint. "Present company excluded, old girl." Damn, now Sophie had him talking to the horses as if they understood.

The sound of approaching footsteps brought an unexpected surge of anticipation. His hopes were dashed when Damon strolled in.

Alex fidgeted with a latch. "I thought you hated it here."

"You were expecting Sophie, I guess. She's already turned in for the night."

Was he so transparent, or was his brother on a fishing expedition? "I was just heading back to the house. Did you want something?"

"I wanted to thank you for taking Sophie riding today. She really had a great time."

"Is that all she said?"

Damon cocked an eyebrow suspiciously. "Was there something else to tell?"

"No. How's the tournament going?"

"Great."

"I'm glad to hear that." Alex clicked the last latch shut. "Considering the club's tournament doesn't begin until next month."

Damon didn't have the decency to look embarrassed. He shrugged and twisted the toe of his Gucci loafer against the concrete floor. The grating sound made the horses shift in their stalls. "Are you going to tell her?"

"Is that what you want me to do? Make a problem between the two of you?"

"No," Damon tossed out without conviction.

"Why lie? I thought the two of you had some great relationship where you each pursue your own interests separately. At least that's how she explains your long absences."

"You wouldn't understand."

"You're right." Alex folded his arms across his chest and leaned his shoulder into the wall. "And

I'm not sure I want to. You seem to make a habit of lying to her.''

"I suppose it's your brotherly loyalty that stops you from telling her the truth?''

"No. It's because you want me to tell her, and until I know why, I'm staying out of this entire affair.''

Damon grinned enigmatically. "That might be difficult.''

"Oh? And why is that?''

"Because the little Gypsy has a way of weaving a spell over a man that makes him want to protect her and make her his own.'' Damon backed out of the stable, pausing at the door. "Which, by the way, is the last thing in the world she wants. Take it from someone who learned the hard way.''

The ring of genuine anguish in Damon's voice as he walked away didn't fool Alex for a second. His stepbrother had never cared about another person in his life.

"What next?'' he wondered aloud as he finished closing the stable for the night. Damon had all but admitted that Sophie wasn't his fiancée. So why wouldn't she admit it? What did she have to gain by keeping up the pretense?

Alex groaned. He had too many questions and not nearly enough answers.

Five

Sophie tiptoed along the narrow curb, imitating the tightrope walkers she had admired as a child. She loved the early morning, a passion she didn't share with the occupants of The Sanctuary. Or the fine citizens of Fairfield, Connecticut. She'd been trying to hitch a ride for the past twenty minutes and not a single car had passed. Had she stepped into the twilight zone? She had visions of arriving in the town center to find a ghost town.

Sunday in the suburbs. If the quiet didn't kill her, the boredom would. The only excitement she'd come across since her arrival was a man she should definitely avoid, but even leaving his house hadn't helped. She couldn't escape from Alex. He invaded her dreams, her waking thoughts and especially her fantasies.

Was his apparent interest in her related to a grudge

against Damon? Did it matter? She wasn't looking for a lifelong love. In her experience men either tried to put women in a cage or they left when they couldn't. Her own father was a prime example.

The sound of an engine humming gave her a start. She had given up hope of finding signs of life. Settling her oversize handbag on her shoulder, she stuck out her thumb. A shiny black Blazer came to a halt alongside her. As the power window lowered slowly, she leaned against the passenger door.

Alex's less-than-cheery face greeted her.

"Oh, no," she grumbled.

"What the hell are you doing?"

"Hitching a ride to town."

"If you wanted to go somewhere, why didn't you ask?"

"I didn't realize I needed your permission to go out."

"That's not what I meant." He leaned across the seat and opened the door. "Get in."

"I'll wait for the next car to pass by."

"It's a private road. You might not see another car for hours."

She rolled her eyes. "Are you going into town?"

"Yes."

"All right." She slipped into the seat and remained completely still as Alex pulled the seat belt across her body. His fingers brushed over her thigh. A sigh escaped before she could suppress it.

He smiled. "You could have asked to borrow a car if you wanted to go somewhere."

"I'm not quite so presumptuous."

"It's a car, for crying out loud, not an organ donation."

Apparently Alex didn't have a love affair with his automobiles like most men. Then again, nothing about Alex was typical.

"What are you doing up so early?" she asked casually, while pretending to be interested in the view out the window. It was better than concentrating on the musky scent of him, she thought. And smarter than dwelling on the warm, tingling sensation that overtook her body every time he was near.

"I need oats."

"Looking for fiber? Are you feeling a little bound up?"

He laughed although she could tell he didn't want to. "For the horses. I'm pretty regular, thank you very much."

She couldn't believe they were discussing his intestinal fortitude, but it beat the hell out of rehashing their scene in the stable yesterday. Obviously he had regrets since he had skipped dinner and avoided her the rest of the evening.

"What time does this town spring to life? I feel like I'm in some Vampire Village where the residents only come out at night."

Alex jammed the truck in gear. "Now we're a bunch of bloodsuckers, are we?"

She tossed up her hands in defeat. "I give up. I'm not going to be able to say anything right today."

He exhaled and eased his grip on the stick shift. "I'm sorry. But when I find my houseguest hitchhiking on a deserted road dressed like…" He motioned toward her body.

"What's wrong with my clothes?"

"Let me put it to you this way. I think there's an

ordinance in this conservative town forbidding biker shorts on a female over the age of twelve."

"Heaven forbid, I should do time on a spandex rap." She ran her finger over the edge of her neon pink, midriff shirt. "I suppose the shirt is inappropriate, too."

His lips curved back in a broad grin. "Definitely. Who taught you how to dress?"

"My mama."

He let out a long whistle. "I want to meet your mama."

"Be careful what you wish for. She'll tell you things about yourself you might not want to hear. She has a gift."

"Does she?"

"You think I'm joking. I'm not."

"I believe you." Alex couldn't tear his gaze away from her arresting green eyes. Not five seconds earlier he had wanted to throttle her for putting herself in danger. Her outfit should be outlawed. If she had reached the highway, she would have caused a ten-car pileup of men trying to offer her a ride. She deserved a good lecture, but when he looked at her, talk was the last thing on his mind. He found himself falling under that Gypsy spell Damon had warned him about.

Admit it, chump. Your curiosity has gotten the better of your common sense. You want to get to know her despite the fact that you're playing right into your brother's hands.

"What do you say we stop somewhere for breakfast and then I'll take you on a little tour of the area?"

"I'm sure you have better things to do."

"I can't think of one. Takeout or sit-down?"

"Takeout. The Golden Arches will be fine."

He shrugged and headed out old Route 1. The morning traffic was light, and they made the trip in ten minutes. He pulled the truck up to the speaker and placed the order.

"That will be six dollars and thirty-two cents. Drive through, please," said a scratchy voice.

Sophie rooted through her purse. "My treat."

"No."

"Don't be ridiculous. I'm staying in your house. The least I can do is spring for breakfast."

"Would Damon allow you to pay?"

A smile twitched at the corners of her full lips. "I'd have to. He never carries cash on him."

Alex wasn't surprised. He brought the Blazer to a halt at the pickup window. A teenage girl pushed open the glass and held out her hand. Before he could reach for his wallet, Sophie unlocked her seat belt and vaulted from her seat, landing across his lap. Using the door for leverage, she slid herself halfway out the open window and handed the money to the cashier.

Wedged between the steering wheel and his chest, Sophie's cute little derriere wiggled forward. With his arms pinned down, he had no choice but to let her pay. Her spandex shorts revealed every muscle of her well-toned thighs, rounded bottom and narrow waist. While the view might be great, her taunting laugh of triumph pushed him too far. He lowered his head and playfully nipped her fleshy back cheek.

She let out a yelp and quickly slid back into her seat. "What's the big idea?"

"You mean that wasn't the breakfast you were offering me?"

"You're a sore loser." She rubbed her hand over her rear end, at the same time fighting back a smile.

He took the paper sack of food from the giggling teenager and handed it to Sophie. "And you play dirty."

"I play to win."

On that point he had no doubt, but was she playing a game he wanted her to win, or one he couldn't afford to lose? She was not some innocent ingenue unaware of what she was doing to him. She was tied to his brother in some way. Perhaps not in the way he had been led to believe, but some sense of loyalty had stopped her from telling him the truth yesterday.

"There's a nature trail a few miles from here. Do you feel like hiking or would you prefer a museum?"

"Hiking." She removed a sausage biscuit from the bag, peeled back half the paper and handed the sandwich to him.

"Thanks."

"Any time." She took a sandwich for herself and settled into the seat while he made the fifteen-minute drive to the preserve.

Alex parked the truck on the side of the road near a wooden bridge. As Sophie collected her large carpetbag purse and slipped outside, he searched the back seat for his old college sweatshirt.

"You better wear this," he said when he joined her.

Her eyes flashed with anger. "Are you embarrassed to be seen with me?"

"No. Ever hear of Lyme disease? I can't do much

about your legs except check thoroughly for ticks when we leave.''

"Oh," she mumbled. Her next words were cut off as she pulled the fleece shirt over her head. She freed her hair from the neckline and gave her head a shake. A halo of sable brown curls framed her face.

He liked the image of her wearing his clothes more than he should.

"Yale?" she noted, running her fingertip over the embossed lettering. He felt a misplaced envy for the letters *Y* and *E* that rested on the peaks of her breasts.

"Something wrong with Yale?"

"No. I guess the commute was easy."

"I lived on campus. I needed to get out."

Sophie skipped ahead and stepped onto the footbridge. "So, the walls get to you, too."

"Only when I let them."

She rested her back against the rail and stretched her legs across the width so he had no choice but to step over her to pass. "It must be nice to have so much control over your emotions. In my family, we tend to be volatile with ours. It's all very dramatic."

Alex grinned as he moved over her. He had seen a hint of those *volatile emotions* in the stable yesterday. "Are you close to your family?"

"Sure. I don't see my mother as often as I'd like, but my grandmother is nearby and I visit her at least once a week. Except in the summer when she spends a few months traveling with the carnival."

"She must be getting on in years."

"She's only in her early sixties. My mother had me when she was sixteen. Most people think she's my older sister. And most times she acts like my younger sister."

He draped his arm across her shoulders. "Does that bother you?"

She paused for a moment before answering. "It used to. Now I accept her for who she is."

"And who is that?"

"The woman who gave me life. Who taught me the value of freedom, the importance of self-reliance and who gave me every child's dream of running off with the circus, so to speak. That is, until some family-court judge stuck his nose in."

"What about your father? Didn't he object?"

He noted the sparks of anger that danced in her eyes. "He wasn't exactly rushing forward to claim his paternal rights where I was concerned."

They walked along the well-marked trail. "Hell of a way to grow up, always moving around."

"Actually I had a great childhood. I love *carnie* people. They live life, not just pass through it. I got a better education on the road than I ever got in public school. Some things can't be learned from a book."

"I guess I don't have the right to judge."

"You don't. It's not something a *gadjo* can understand."

"A what?"

"*Gadjo.* It's Romany for anyone who's not a Gypsy. Like my grandmother, I still enjoy hooking up with the carnival for a few weeks every summer. I read cards, sketch the townies and dance until the sun comes up."

"I bet you're a hit with the locals."

She kicked at a pebble. "I don't dance for an audience. Only friends."

"Then I'll consider myself lucky that I got to see you."

She smiled. "Heck of an icebreaker, huh?"

"An ice melter," he muttered.

As they hiked, he continued to ask her questions about her interesting—albeit, unorthodox—childhood among the urban Gypsies. Although she answered each query, she rarely volunteered information. Wisely, he steered clear of the subject of Damon. He didn't want to put her in a position where she might lie to him.

They followed the trail to a waterfall. A clear pool formed at the bottom, surrounded by large boulders. Sophie crouched down on a flat granite rock and tossed stones into the water, sending ripples across the surface.

"Well, that was Sophie Anders, The Early Years. Did you learn everything you needed to know?"

Not nearly as much as he wanted to, he thought as he sat down next to her. "Do you want to stay here for a while?"

"You probably have things to do today." She started to get up.

He grabbed the back of her sweatshirt and hauled her into his lap. Her eyes widened and she let out a startled gasp.

"If I had something to do, I'd tell you. And I didn't mean to sound as if I was interrogating you."

Sophie willed her body to remain calm, but her brain had ceded power to her hormones and they had taken control with a vengeance. A ripple of heat flowed through her. She could blame her reaction on his intoxicating scent or on the warmth generated by the expanse of his broad chest as he cradled her close. Hell, why not blame the moon as well? Anything was better than admitting how much she wanted this man.

Alex obviously wanted her, too. He hadn't gone out of his way to hide his desire for her. Or his distrust. A distrust he had every reason to feel. She silently cursed Damon for putting her in this position, but she was as much to blame for perpetuating the lie.

Tilting her head back, she gazed into his eyes. She was free to tell him the truth and then they could move on with their relationship. Why did she hold back?

She would only be here until the end of the week. Did she really want to get in any deeper? Could she stop herself? If her feelings for him were purely physical, she could deal with an affair. But her emotions were becoming involved. Alex touched her in a place no one else had been able to reach before— her heart.

She rested her head on his shoulder, his cotton T-shirt caressing her cheek as she snuggled closer. "Obsession," she muttered.

His deep chuckle vibrated against her ear. "Is that a fact?"

"No. It's your cologne." And aptly named, she decided.

On reflection, she knew very little about Alex, and what she did know came from Damon, who proved he hadn't been honest with her. She thought about Alex's engagement and an uncustomary blast of jealousy followed. Why? He hadn't reached the age of thirty-two without a few relationships behind him.

She'd had a few herself. Still, he had loved another woman enough to propose marriage.

"What's wrong?"

She shook her head. "What makes you ask?"

"You're tense."

"I have a lot on my mind." *Like guilt, confusion, and fear—and not necessarily in that order.*

"Maybe you need something to distract you." He slid his hand under the floppy sweatshirt and splayed his fingers over her stomach. The tickling sensation caused her muscles to contract. "Are you distracted?"

"Oh yeah." She let out an exhalation of air. "But I don't think you'll relieve my tension like that."

"Maybe this will help." He cupped her breast, rubbing his thumb over the hardened nipple. A breath caught in her throat as he continued to stroke the sensitive area. "I know it's helping me to relax."

A hunger burned inside her, aching for release. She wrapped her arms around his neck and gave into the mind-numbing escape of purely physical pleasure.

He slipped his hand around to her back, drawing her closer. His mouth covered hers, muffling her eager sigh. Heat pulsed through her. His tongue swept over her parted lips then pushed inside her mouth. The feel of him, the taste of him, so all-consuming, far outweighed any reservations she had about getting involved.

She ran her fingers through his silken hair. Wiggling in his lap, she felt the evidence of his desire pressing against her hip. A deep groan vibrated in her ear. The barrier of clothing became an uncomfortable hindrance. She reached for the buttons on Alex's shirt, popping the first two easily.

A loud wolf whistle pierced the summer silence. With a frustrated moan, she dropped her hand to her lap. Alex drew back reluctantly, tugging her sweatshirt back into place. He brushed away the tangle of hair from her cheek and gave her one more kiss. A group of teenagers walking along the footpath sent them a cheer. Alex nodded sheepishly, but Sophie, never one to let someone else have the upper hand, stood up and took a bow. They applauded her soundly.

"Sorry, guys. The next performance will be for a private audience." After a few boos and jeers, the boys continued on their way. "I guess it wasn't a bright idea to start necking in a public park."

"It wasn't a bright idea at all." Regret resonated in his voice. He refastened his buttons. His eyes were narrowed and impossible to read.

Refusing to let him see how deeply his words cut, she drew in a long breath and smiled. "You're right. We should get going."

He came to his feet. "Look, Sophie, I'm not blaming you. I only meant—"

"Your meaning was clear." Whether he blamed her or himself didn't matter. He regretted the kiss.

"Then tell me I'm wrong. Tell me I have no reason to feel guilty."

How could she tell him what to feel, when she had no idea how to deal with her own emotions? She couldn't remember a time when she wanted something so badly. Or when she was so frightened by that desire. How could she be losing her heart to a man who was the antithesis of everything she held dear?

Alex had roots. He planned his life beyond the next full moon. She had never signed a lease because the idea of being tied to anything for a year made her crazy. She didn't own a credit card, had never taken a loan, and the only commitment she'd ever made was to her education.

"You didn't answer me."

"You didn't ask a question."

"And you don't volunteer information unless you're asked."

She raked her fingers through her hair. "Right."

"Well, I'm not going to ask." His angular jaw was set in solid determination.

"Then I'd say we've reached a stalemate."

"I prefer to call it a standoff. We'll see who can hold out longer."

Sexual blackmail. She would laugh if he hadn't read her so well. Ironic, since she was the one who usually had insights into people. Yet, for all the thought she gave him, Alex remained an enigma. Squaring her shoulders, she started walking down the path.

"You coming?" she called over her shoulder. "Or should I hitchhike back?"

Alex broke out in a wide grin and followed behind her. He suspected she exaggerated the sway in her hips to torment him. She needn't have bothered. His body was still aroused from their kiss. Sophie had responded to the slightest touch with unrestrained hunger, and she had nearly sent him over the edge. For a man who prided himself on his self-control, the experience had been humbling.

Without warning, she began to sprint through the trees like a gazelle in flight. Leaves crunched as her sneakers made contact with the ground. He didn't try to catch up. Whatever compelled her to run was something she had to work out for herself. He already knew what he wanted. He wanted Sophie, and not just for an affair.

When he reached the Blazer, she was leaning against the passenger door. A mass of tousled curls framed her face, flushed from the physical exertion. Her chest rose and fell as she drew in deep gulps of air.

"Feel better?" he asked.

"Great," she grumbled breathlessly.

"Good. Give me your left leg."

"What?"

"I have to check for ticks."

"Check with your eyes."

He cupped his hand beneath the bend of her knee. "It's more thorough this way."

She hopped once and grabbed onto the door handle. With slow, deliberate movements, he ran his fingers over the bare skin along her calf, over her kneecap and up to the edge of her Lycra shorts.

A tiny bump stopped his probing on her inner thigh.

Sophie trembled slightly. "It's a beauty mark."

"And a lovely one at that." He grinned and repeated the process on the other leg.

"Are you finished?" she said through clenched teeth.

"I don't know. Your sweatshirt was up above your waist for a while. Maybe I should—"

"Forget it." She slapped his hand away.

He shrugged. "Just trying to help."

"Yeah, right," she mumbled.

Alex chuckled. She wasn't going to last much longer. He admired her determination. He even respected her sense of loyalty to Damon. But unless she admitted the truth before they went any further, their relationship would have no future because it would be built on a foundation of lies.

During the ride home, Sophie pretended to be asleep. When he stopped for horse feed, she showed all the response of a comatose victim. But as soon as he cut the engine back at the estate, she sprung to life.

"I'm going to take Elvis for a ride," she announced as she jumped from the truck.

He caught up to her in the stable. "Take Delilah. She hasn't had a good run in a while."

She nodded. "Okay."

"Do you want me to come?"

"No. I need to be alone for a while."

He caught her wrist as she turned, tugging her against his chest. Her eyes rounded in surprise. He brushed a kiss across her mouth, flicking his tongue over her lips before quickly releasing her. "Try not to miss me while you're gone."

Six

Sophie fastened a towel around her damp body. Her earlier ride on Delilah and the long hot shower afterward hadn't worked out the frustration she felt. *Try not to miss me.* As if she had a choice.

She took her silver bangles from the sink and put them on. This was one of those moments when she wished she could talk to her mother. Natalie Anders—or Madam Nadia, as she liked to be known—had a way of making Sophie put things in perspective. Not that they ever agreed on how to proceed.

What would Natalie advise? *Live and let tomorrow take care of itself.* Her mother would never understand her misgivings. Of course, Natalie had had more lovers than birthdays and never lost her heart to any of them. Sophie had always believed that was her destiny, too, and she'd deliberately dated men who were emotionally cold. That way she could walk away without guilt and never get hurt. Somehow, she didn't believe she would be able to walk away from Alex unscathed. And she wasn't sure she wanted to.

She dragged a comb through her tangled curls. Once she told Alex the truth, would he still want her? Did he have feelings for her, or was he only looking to settle a score? Would he be interested in continuing their relationship after they left The Sanctuary? With so many doubts lingering, the last thing she should be contemplating was the course of action she knew irrefutably she would take.

She applied scented oil to her pulse points. The exotic mixture had been rumored among the Gypsies to drive men wild although she had never put the concoction to the test before. Her stomach clenched into a tight knot. She dressed in a pair of red lace panties and the flannel shirt she'd swiped from Alex's room a few minutes earlier. Wrapping her arms around herself, she let his masculine scent envelop her. The earthy smell gave her a boost of courage.

With Damon and his mother at the country club and the cook already gone for the day, Sophie only had to elude the aging butler as she tiptoed through the quiet house. As she made her way across the yard to the stable, she saw no sign of Alex. His truck was still in the driveway so he couldn't have left. One by one, she led the horses to the paddock. Eventually, he would have to investigate why the animals were outside.

While she waited inside, Sophie tied a leather strap through a gate slat and made a loop at the end. She twisted a knot as complicated as the tangled mess she had made with one small lie. If Alex wanted honesty, she'd give him all the honesty he could handle. And then some. Her palms felt damp and she wiped them against her shirt. The jangle of her bracelets echoed off the walls.

At the sound of approaching footsteps, she inhaled deeply. "Why are the horses out—" Alex's words cut off abruptly. "What are you doing?"

She expelled the breath she'd been holding. "I'm not engaged to Damon. We're not even involved."

A silent pause hung between them. Why didn't he say something? Wasn't that what he'd wanted to hear? She fidgeted with the piece of leather rather than turn to face him.

"Are you going to tie me up with that and have your way with me?" he asked.

"No." She slipped her hands through the loop and pulled until the knot tightened around her wrists.

"You're wearing my shirt," he noted.

"I told you us Gypsies are notorious thieves."

He cleared his throat. "You wearing anything underneath?"

She turned slowly. The shirt fell open as she leaned against the wall with her hands above her head.

"Not much," he muttered.

"Are you gonna stand there and gawk? I'm getting cold."

He smiled and took a step closer. His eyes ran a sweeping gaze over the length of her. He reached for the leather restraint.

Sophie shook her head. "No."

"No?"

"I'm not to be trusted." More than that, she wanted him to understand that she trusted him. With her body and with her heart. That much power she had never ceded to anyone.

He arched his eyebrow in confusion. "What does that mean?"

"If you let my hands free, I can't be held responsible for what I might do to you."

She noticed him fighting back a laugh. "So what's your point?"

"With what I want to do, we might be finished before we've begun."

He let out a groan. "Did my brother bring you here to kill me?"

Inching forward, she wrapped one leg around his calf and urged him closer. "Do we have to discuss Damon?"

"Just as long as he's not the reason you're here now."

"My reasons have nothing to do with Damon, and everything to do with you."

Her answer seemed to satisfy him. He brushed a kiss across her cheek. "What do you want me to do?"

"Everything."

"That's a tall order." His hand slipped inside her shirt, molding her breast in his grasp.

A delightful tremor washed over her. "I'm sure you're up—"

He cut off her teasing with a long, hot kiss. She wanted to run her fingers through his hair, hold him close. She tugged, but her wrists were firmly bound. Arching forward, she brushed against his worn jeans. Oh, yes. He was up for it, all right.

He caught her earlobe in his teeth, nipping at the tiny silver earring. She sighed and tilted her head back against the wall. Featherlight kisses fluttered over her neck and throat. A ribbon of heat unraveled in her belly. He took her breast into his mouth, sucking until the nipple throbbed.

Sophie muttered something, but she wasn't sure what. She hoped she wouldn't regret the words later. If Alex heard he must have been pleased because she felt his lips form a smile as he worked his tongue over her rib cage. Tremors, warm and wonderful, danced along her spine.

Alex dropped to his knees. Hooking the elastic waistband with his thumbs, he slid her satin panties over her hips, then let them fall to the ground.

"Apricot," he muttered as he tasted the skin along her upper thigh.

"It's supposed to drive a man wild," she said on a rush of air.

"Does the rest of you taste as good?"

"Find out."

Alex took up the challenge and her giggles quickly faded to a moan. He ran his hand along her calf then lifted her leg onto his shoulder. He glanced up at her and she was lost. Warm kisses, a heated touch and fire in the depth of his gorgeous brown eyes conspired to send her over the edge too soon.

She felt herself slipping, losing control. "Oh, no."

"Oh, yes." Alex's voice came out in a husky groan. He stroked his finger over her navel then down into the damp hair between her thighs.

Bracing her back against the wall, she raised her hips as he probed the sensitive area around her center core. He separated the folds of skin and closed his mouth over the pulsing nub.

A jolt of electricity shot straight through her. She

tightened her grip on the leather strap and closed her eyes, giving in to the exquisite pleasure.

Alternating between flicking his tongue and sucking with greedy hunger, he unleashed a tidal wave that sent her crashing. Spasms rocked her body. Her strangled cry of release echoed off the high walls.

She struggled for a normal breath. Her climax was more than physical. Alex reached her on an emotional plane, touching a part of her that was previously uncharted. She knew she should worry, but she felt too damn good right now to think about the implications.

He rose, palming her swollen breasts and kissing her deeply. His lopsided grin bordered on cocky, but he'd certainly earned the right to gloat.

Alex loosened the leather strap and slid it off Sophie's wrists. She collapsed against him, flexing her cramped muscles. Her bracelets chimed.

"Are you all right?"

She shrugged and nuzzled closer. "A bit sore."

He massaged her upper arms. "Why didn't you say something?"

She smiled, her body still shuddering. "I didn't notice at the time."

"Let's go back to the house."

"No way. I have a little score to settle."

He arched an eyebrow and grinned. "I didn't realize you'd feel the need for revenge."

She fumbled with his belt buckle. "Liar. You were counting on it."

Alex swallowed a chuckle. He'd never met a woman who thoroughly enjoyed being touched the way Sophie did. Every stroke, every gesture, brought a moan or a sigh. She was easy to arouse, easy to please. He wondered if she would be so easy to hold on to, because he knew he would never be able to let her go.

He grabbed the lapels of her flannel shirt—his shirt. "Protection's in the house."

"It's in my pocket," she muttered against his ear, refusing to be deterred from her course of action. "When I plan a seduction, I don't leave anything to chance."

She had covered all her bases. To a point where he no longer cared why she had come here in the first place. Chaos was descending on his orderly world and he welcomed the upheaval.

The exotic taste of apricot still lingered and left him hungry for more. He glanced around the stable, looking for a soft area. Sophie, one step ahead, found a wool horse blanket and draped it over the bales of hay. He eyed the result suspiciously.

"It'll work. Trust me." She drew up in front of him and worked his T-shirt over his head. He tried to help, but she pushed his hand away. "Hey, it's my turn, and I'm in no hurry."

He was already aroused to the point of pain. "It's not necessary—"

"Oh, but it is. One very good turn deserves another."

The hoarsely whispered words shot through him.

She kneaded the muscles along his chest in a slow, circular motion, lulling him into a false sense of security. He kicked off one sneaker, then the other.

"I told you, it's my turn. I say what comes off and when." Her fingernail scored a line across his torso. He struggled for a breath. The woman *was* safer with her hands tied.

He had never worried about his stamina before, but he seriously wondered today if he would be able to keep up with his unrestrained and inexhaustible partner. She didn't have a reserved bone in her body. As a romantic setting, the stable ranked dead last on his list of hot spots, but he guessed she preferred here to the house she found so oppressive.

Her wide eyes and angelic face were misleading. She was neither helpless nor gentle. In fact, she got downright physical while trying to divest him from his jeans.

"Would you slow down?" he said with a laugh.

"Did I comment on your technique?"

"Did you have a complaint?" he countered.

She pressed her palm against his shoulder and urged him onto the makeshift sofa. After pulling off his jeans and tossing them carelessly to the ground, she wriggled herself between his legs and dropped to her knees on the pile of denim.

"Make yourself comfortable. This might take a while." She splayed her fingers over his chest and tugged at the mat of coarse hair.

"Is this some Gypsy brand of torture?"

Her smile broadened. "Absolutely." Her hand roamed lower, cupping his hard shaft in a surprisingly strong grip. He jerked in response.

With a mischievous glint in her eyes she stroked him repeatedly. Her bracelets jingled like sleigh bells. It was Christmas in July—and he was getting one heck of a present.

"You're playing with fire now," he growled.

"Do you want me to stop?"

"No way." He squeezed his eyes shut and mentally tried counting to retain control. A feat that became nearly impossible when she lowered her head and intimately kissed the pulsing tip of his erection and flickered her tongue along the length. Her hair spilled over his thighs. He buried his hands into the mass of curls and brought her head up.

"I want to be inside you."

"I'm all for that." She removed a foil packet from her pocket then let the shirt slip from her shoulders. "Should I?" she asked, holding up the condom.

"Be my guest." He would probably embarrass himself if he tried in his present impatient state. However, once she took on the task with painfully slow and provocative precision he questioned his wisdom. "Enough, Sophie."

She straddled his lap, rubbing her breasts against his chest. As he pushed inside her, she drew in a deep breath and let out a contented sigh.

"Umm," she mumbled.

His sentiments exactly. She was so hot, so tight and wet with desire for him. He gave her a moment to center herself before moving beneath her.

He gripped her waist, raising her up and bringing her down to meet each thrust. She matched his rhythm. No, she set the rhythm. Fast, furious, beyond the ability to control. Their bodies, covered with a fine sheen of perspiration, moved together with tantalizing ease.

His heart raced. He kissed her deeply, hoping to momentarily distract her. His plan backfired. When his tongue swept over her lips, her muscles contracted around him.

She wrapped her arms around his neck and gave into the tremors that racked her body. Her climax precipitated his own. He drove into her one last time, triggering a release so powerful, he was half-afraid he would hurt her.

Fingernails dug into his flesh. A breath caught in her throat, causing a soft whimper to escape. He glanced up in time to catch her astonished expression.

He brushed a finger over her lips. She caught it between her teeth and laved the tip. A tear spilled over her cheek. "What's this?"

She shook her head.

The sun had dropped below the horizon and a light evening breeze stirred the humid air in the stable. Sophie's body glistened in the muted lighting. Her chest rose and fell as she struggled for a normal breath. Alex stroked her hair until she purred and snuggled against him. Something had happened between them, and it was more than good sex.

A few events in his life had been memorable for various reasons. His kidnapping as a child. The unexpected death of his father. Both of those incidents had fostered a need to protect the people around him—not always to a positive end. Again he felt the fierce desire to shelter and protect. He remembered Damon's warning.

It's the last thing in the world she wants.

How could he hold on to a free spirit without making her feel caged?

How could he let her go?

Sophie felt Alex's arms tense around her. His brows furrowed in serious thought. Regret? She certainly hoped not.

He had surprised her in more ways than one. Not once, but twice, he had sent her over the edge. And she had thought multiple orgasms only occurred in fiction. That would teach her to prejudge. She had expected him to be conservative and straitlaced when it came to sex. Instead, the man had made her cry. No one would ever be able to top that.

She smoothed a finger over his eyebrow. "Where are you, Alex?"

His gaze locked on hers. For a long moment he stared blankly, then shook his head and grinned. "I'm still inside you."

She exhaled a puff of air. "Typical male. Should we go up to the house?"

"I'll meet you there in five minutes. I have to let the horses back in."

"I'll help."

"No. I can handle it."

"Okay." She tried not to show her disappointment. Apparently he wanted some distance.

She slid off him and grabbed the shirt from the ground. As she began to push her arm through the twisted fabric, Alex came up from behind and gave her a hand. He rested his chin on her shoulder and fastened the buttons.

"I just need five minutes to catch my breath. Don't start anything until I get there." He punctuated his request with a nip to her earlobe.

Damn! How could he read her so well when she couldn't figure him out at all?

She sprinted to the house and sneaked up the back stairs to her bedroom. Outside the window, a deep purple sky was fading to black. She picked through her suitcase for a candle to take into the master bathroom, which consisted of a white-tiled room with glass-encased shower and Jacuzzi.

After filling the sunken tub with hot water, she poured in a capful of scented oil. The smell of lavender filled the room. She stripped off her shirt and lowered herself into the bath. A blanket of warmth enveloped her. The pulsing jets massaged her body, making her skin tingle as it had minutes before. She leaned her head against the rim and let out a loud sigh.

"I thought I told you not to start without me," Alex called from his bedroom.

She slapped her hand on the enamel surface. "When you have one of these babies, who needs a man?"

He stepped into the candlelit bathroom, holding a bottle of wine and two crystal glasses. "Can I interest you?"

She ran an appraising gaze over his naked body and smiled mischievously. "You're supposed to get me drunk first, then have your way with me."

"I like to do things the hard way." He poured two glasses of wine and handed one to her. "Move up."

He slid in behind her, settling her between his thighs. She wriggled against him. He wrapped his legs around her waist to still her and draped his arm across her chest.

"Comfortable?"

"Positively spoiled," she muttered.

"Good. Because I have a few questions I want to ask about your arrangement with Damon. Or did you think this seduction scene would distract me?"

"I had hoped." She took a sip of the dry wine. "You might want to drink down that glass before I start. You're not gonna like it."

"Nothing he does would surprise me."

"Damon and I have been friends for a long time." She took another gulp for courage and rested her glass on the floor. "He asked me for a favor. To pretend to be his fiancée. No one was supposed to get hurt."

"But why you?"

"He said you and his mother were after him about getting married, so he wanted to bring home a woman who was totally inappropriate, and I fit the bill."

His laughter tickled her neck. "I wouldn't wish him on any woman."

"He's not so bad. Okay, so he's not marriage material, but he's been there for me when I've needed him. He's helped me move. Several times. He gave me my first graphic design job, which led to several others."

She debated telling him what she'd learned only after her arrival. Bringing up Alex's ex-fiancée while his hand gently stroked her breast seemed poor timing at best, and just plain crass. Would he believe that her reasons for being with him had nothing to do with his brother's attempt to even a score?

"So you owed him."

"It's more than that. He offered to make a donation to a youth center where I volunteer if I helped him out."

"By coming here and seducing his brother?"

"Hey, don't blame him for that. Seducing you was my idea. If you'd been an uptight, stuffy snob like you were supposed to be, none of this would have happened."

His fingers drummed playfully over her stomach. "Is that a fact?"

She shrugged. "Probably not. But it would have taken longer to get us here."

"I doubt it." Alex tightened his hold around her.

He would have to be dead before he could control the physical reactions Sophie inspired. The scent of her, the taste, was enough to drive a man to distraction. He knew there was more to Damon's plan than she'd told him. His brother didn't have enough money to make more than a token donation to charity. Unless, of course, Alex agreed to divide the trust. Did she know the entire story?

"Sophie?"

"Umm." The soft purring sound vibrated against his chest. Was she tired or hoping to avoid further questions? He came to his feet, lifting her up with him. The answers would wait another day.

She groaned in protest as he lowered her to the floor. "Something I said?"

He pulled a bath sheet from the brass rack and folded it around her trembling body. "I thought we'd be more comfortable in my bedroom."

"You might be." She shook her head, sending a spray of water around the bathroom. Damp strands of hair sprung into spiral curls around her face.

"You weren't planning to stay the night with me?"

"I'm not used to sleeping with anyone. I might keep you awake all night."

He cocked an eyebrow suggestively. "I'm counting on it."

A moan escaped through her tightly pursed lips. She tapped her bare foot in a small puddle of water on the tile floor. "I'm not joking."

"Neither am I, Sophie." He rubbed the towel over

her shoulders and arms. Her satiny skin had a healthy pink glow.

"Why?"

"Call me old-fashioned but I wouldn't have made love to you if I didn't want you to spend the night with me."

"I snore and kick," she warned as he urged her toward the bedroom.

"I'll risk it."

She hesitated at the door as if her body and her mind were having a clash of wills. "Okay, but if you're suffering from sleep deprivation in the morning, don't blame me."

Her reluctant agreement felt like a victory. He wouldn't allow her to separate her emotions from her actions. Her Gypsy childhood had taught her too much self-reliance and independence for her own good. Sophie needed to learn to share.

She pointed to the king-size bed. "Do you prefer the right side or left side?"

"I'm easy."

"That's what you think," she mumbled.

He cupped his fingers over her slender neck and edged her toward him. "You're making a big deal out of nothing."

Eyes as dark as jade met his gaze. "It isn't nothing or you wouldn't have insisted."

"You're right." He held back the sheets and waited for her to crawl in. Before she could scramble to the far side of the bed, he slipped in and snaked his arm around her waist. Her velvety skin warmed him.

She wriggled restlessly. The rapid beat of her heart drummed against his fingertips and he could almost believe she was afraid of him. Why? She certainly hadn't had any reservations when they were in the stable.

"Do you want me to put the television on?"

She turned on her side. "If you want."

"What I want is for you to relax and give this a chance. You might actually enjoy sleeping with me instead of alone."

"I know," she murmured against his ear.

"Then what's the problem?"

"That is the problem."

He grinned and snuggled her into the crook of his shoulder. Despite her earlier hesitation, she relaxed and cuddled around him. Her eyelids fluttered closed. She pressed her lips against his chest, then nipped at his flesh.

His body grew hard and he realized he wasn't going to get much sleep with her next to him. He felt rather than saw her triumphant smile. While he might have won the first round tonight, she had by no means thrown in the towel.

Seven

Wrapped in a sheet, Sophie sat by the window and thumbed through her sketch pad. Muscles she didn't know she possessed ached with the glorious feeling of fulfillment. She tucked her hair behind her ear and glanced toward the bed. Charcoal in hand, she began to sketch Alex's magnificent naked form. He would most likely be out for a few hours, at least. A smile tugged at her mouth. He'd insisted she spend the night. She only gave him what he'd asked for.

Unfortunately, she got more than she'd bargained for in the process. A new and frightening emotion. Desire. Not physical, for he had satisfied her craving in that respect. Alex had tapped into her heart and left her with the longing to be more to him than a vacation fling. But where did she fit into his orderly, structured life? They lived in different states, different worlds. He'd made no promises and she'd asked for none.

Smooth move, Sophie. That's what you get for not listening to your mama.

She should have known that Alex was trouble the moment she went crashing into him. No, she knew before coming to The Sanctuary, but she'd ignored the warnings in the cards, in the tea leaves. Why?

A feeling of restlessness settled over her. She tossed down her sketch pad and rose from the seat. A brisk ride would clear her muddled thoughts. She plucked a yellow rose from a vase on the desk and laid it on the pillow next to Alex, then left through the bathroom door that connected his room to hers.

She dressed in jeans and Alex's Yale sweatshirt and slipped quietly out the kitchen door. The grass shone with a fine layer of dew. The air smelled sweet and clean. She pushed her sleeves up to her elbows and strode across the driveway toward the stables.

The jangle of keys caught her attention and she turned to see Damon near the garage. She smiled and waved to him.

"Hey, Soph." Seeing Damon up and about before noon was a surprise. He crossed the lawn and joined her.

"Just getting home?" she teased.

"No. I'm taking my mother to a charity breakfast at the club."

Thankful that he didn't plan to break routine and spend the day with her, she exhaled in relief. She raised a hand to her forehead to shield her eyes from the morning sun. "I'm glad to see you're getting out and around on your vacation."

He grinned knowingly. "I guess you are, too."

"Meaning?"

"I came up to talk to you when I got back last night. Guess what?"

"What?" she asked innocently.

"You weren't in your room."

"I wasn't? You should have checked the salon. There was a good movie on TV last night."

"You expect me to believe that a woman who doesn't own an 'idiot box' on principle was glued to a movie? Nice try, but I did check. As a matter of fact, the only place I didn't check was Alex's room."

She shrugged and said nothing.

"Come on, Soph, you're wearing his clothes."

She slid her hands in her pockets and leaned against the paddock fence. "Butt out, Damon."

"I guess you told him about our nonexistent engagement."

She nodded.

"Was he upset with me?"

"He wasn't surprised." A small laugh escaped. "Did you think we'd fooled him at all?"

Damon hunched his shoulders sheepishly. "No."

"Look. I'm sorry things didn't work out how you'd hoped, but that's what happens when you mess around in other people's lives."

He leaned against the wooden rail next to her. "So, what now? Are you going to stick around awhile after I leave?"

"I plan to hook up with my mother for a few days. Besides, I have work and an apartment to return to next week."

"What about Alex?"

"We didn't discuss it. But he doesn't live here anyway."

Damon ran a sweeping gaze over the landscape. "I don't know why he bothers to hold on to the place. The upkeep is outrageous. And, except for the horses, I don't think he likes the place. Too many bad memories."

She placed a hand on his arm. "Maybe he holds on to it for your mother and you."

"We don't want it. My mother prefers Florida, and I'm a city dweller at heart."

"Why don't you tell him?"

He cocked his head to the side and frowned. "Tell him what, Soph? 'Hey, Alex. We hate your family home.' His father was good to my mother and me. I'm selfish, but even I have my limits."

"I see your point. Well, it's nice to have a place to come home to."

He crinkled his nose in distaste. "It's a mausoleum. That's why I'm at the club all day long."

She couldn't disagree, although the area outside the walls was beautiful. Sprawling farms, unspoiled woodlands and quiet suburban neighborhoods all in a thirty-mile radius. "I don't know what to tell you."

"If he wants to work twenty-hour days so he can maintain the place, that's his choice. But he'd be a lot happier and less stressed if he stopped worrying about us and got his own life instead."

"That's just a part of his nature, Damon." The part that troubled her.

"Well, Mother is waiting." Damon popped a friendly kiss on her forehead and walked back to the house. She watched until he disappeared inside, then continued across the lawn toward the stable.

Her emotions were in a jumble. While he meant well, Alex did try to control the people in his life.

She thought about his subtle, but judgmental comments about her clothes. His insistence that she sleep in his bed last night. His anger when he'd discovered her hitchhiking yesterday. Although, deep down, she knew it had been foolish even in this picture-postcard town.

Was Damon hoping that Alex would take to running her life and leave the rest of his family alone? Could she live with restrictions on her freedom and not start to resent him? For most of her childhood she'd had no real male influences. No father, brother or uncles to watch out for her. Although the carnival community worked as one large family, most children grew up in a carefree, do-as-you-please world.

In contrast, Alex lived in a world of structure, governed by rules and maintained by routine. Opposites might attract, but they didn't always make for a harmonious relationship. She shook her head, determined not to worry about tomorrow.

"Oh, Elvis, what do you say we rock and roll?" she called out as she stepped inside the stable. The horse whinnied and nudged at the gate. Apparently Elvis needed to run free for a while, too.

Alex stretched his arm out across the bed. The cool sheet greeted him. He opened his eyes and saw the rose on the pillowcase. The velvet petals were a poor substitute for Sophie's soft body. He flexed his muscles, tight from the night of lovemaking. At least he knew she hadn't left much before sunrise. He rose from the bed and walked to the window.

As he glanced outside, he saw Damon giving Sophie a kiss. Jealousy caused a knot to form in his stomach. *Get a grip, man. They were friends long before you entered her life.* It was probably nothing more than a friendly gesture.

Refusing to let suspicion cloud his thoughts, he looked away. The sketch pad, lying open on the desk, caught his attention. The drawing of him, sprawled naked across the bed, had excellent detail, but he would have to talk to her about her depth perception concerning certain parts of his anatomy. With a chuckle, he closed the tablet and went to dress.

He took the back stairs to the kitchen two at a time. After a quick check of his messages, he went to join Sophie for a morning ride. At the sound of voices in the foyer, he froze.

"Trust me. It's working like a charm," Damon said.

"You're sure she won't screw it up?" Elaine asked skeptically. "She's a bit flighty."

"Believe me, she's perfect..." The words faded in and out as Damon and Elaine moved down the hall. "...better than I'd planned."

"And if you're wrong? Alex is no fool."

"Don't worry...this time, next week...he'll wish he had..." The front door clicked shut, leaving the house in silence.

Alex exhaled the breath he'd been holding and clenched his fingers into tight fists. Hadn't Sophie told Damon the game was up, or was there more to come? Where did Sophie fit into this new attempt to get him to sell the estate and divide the trust? Nothing he'd heard actually proved she was willingly involved in his brother's plan. And Damon wasn't above using friends to achieve his goals.

How much more could he put up with? His father had asked him to look out for his stepfamily—not become their keeper. Five years of Damon's schemes and lies—not to mention Elaine's unrelenting complaints about the estate had made his assigned role even tougher.

He thought about Sophie. Could she have given so much of herself if she was just playing a part? He didn't want to believe she could, but he'd been wrong about a woman before. Had love blinded him to the truth?

Love?

The realization stunned him. Talk about playing right into his brother's hands. If Alex wanted a future with Sophie, he would have to keep his word and sell the estate anyway.

Sophie ran a brush over Elvis's sleek body. The early-morning ride had started her adrenaline pumping, making up for her lack of sleep last night. The horse nuzzled her shoulder. She stroked his neck and led him back to the stall.

As she clicked the latch, a warm tingle ran along her spine. "How long have you been up?"

Alex stepped into the stable and approached her from behind. "How did you know I was here?"

"I felt you."

"You did?" He slid his hands over her waist and pressed his fingers against her stomach.

"Umm. You feel even better in person." She relaxed against his chest. "You just missed Damon and his mother."

"Did you talk to him this morning?"

"Yes."

"About what?"

She frowned. Was that curiosity or suspicion she

heard in his voice? "He wondered why I wasn't in my room last night. I told him to mind his own business."

"Anything else?"

She turned to face him. "Is something on your mind, Alex?"

His eyes narrowed for a brief moment before he shrugged. "No. What would you like to do today?"

"I don't care. Take a ride around the area or check out the shops in town. If you have something to do, I can entertain myself."

He leaned forward, pinning her against the gate. His lips brushed against her temple. "I'd much rather entertain you."

Despite his playful words, she felt the tension in his body. "Maybe we should talk first."

"Let's go for a drive first and talk later."

"Okay," she agreed, trying to hide the concern from her voice. Apparently something was bothering him. And Damon was probably at the root, but until he wanted to discuss the matter, she couldn't force it out of him.

Alex glanced at Sophie sitting cross-legged in the bucket seat with her hands folded together in her lap. She looked the picture of innocence now, but moments ago he had nearly driven off the road when she had decided to catch his attention with that wayward hand of hers. His button-fly jeans still felt uncomfortably tight. That would teach him not to become preoccupied in her presence again.

"Oh, look. There's an open house. Let's go take a look." She leaned forward in the seat and pointed to the For Sale sign hanging from a split-rail fence.

"Why?"

She winked at him. "I thought you might need to stretch your legs. You look a bit tense."

Not tense—hard, he mentally corrected. He stopped the Blazer at the end of the long winding driveway. "Are you looking to buy?"

"Not at present, but it's fun to take a look around anyway." She glanced at him, her bright eyes hopeful. "If you don't want to, I'll go alone."

"I'll go," he said, and drove toward the house. As they got out of the vehicle, a woman greeted them at the door.

"Hello. I'm Melinda Durning, New England Realty." She handed Alex a card.

Sophie stepped forward and smiled brightly. "Hi. I'm Mindy Sue McMurphy, and this is my husband, Norman."

"Are you in the market for a farm?"

Alex opened his mouth to answer when Sophie grabbed his arm. "Norman wants one of those town house condominiums, but after three years of living in a cramped apartment, I told him the kids need room to play."

He marveled at her ability to speak in a convincing Southern accent and worried about her ability to role-play at will.

"How many children do you have?" Melinda asked.

"Three," said Sophie.

"Two," Alex muttered at the same time, to his own surprise.

"Two and a half," Sophie added smoothly, patting her stomach.

Melinda smiled. "I wish I looked that good when I was pregnant."

"Yes, my little Mindy Sue carries well." He forced a smile and placed a hand on her flat stomach. "You'd never know the last one weighed in at ten pounds. Isn't that right, dear?"

Sophie beamed up at him lovingly. "That's right. How large is the property?"

The real-estate agent checked her clipboard. "Six acres. There's the colonial house, the workers' quarters, a stable and a greenhouse out back. Should we begin with the house?"

Alex followed the two chatting women through the old house. Sophie took her time, stopping to inspect the oak paneling, to open the built-in cabinets or to estimate approximate closet space. Her excited muttering and appreciative sighs echoed around the empty rooms. While she inspected, she continued to answer the real-estate agent's questions about her fictitious life.

He shook his head and tried to ignore the women's conversation. Instead, he gave his attention to the house. Intricate woodwork dated the main part of the building to the turn of the century. Despite his affluent background, he found himself drawn to the rustic charm of the place. A narrow staircase led to the upper floor. Three steps creaked.

Melinda stepped aside to let them enter a bedroom. "The bedrooms are small but there's potential. These two could be opened up to a master suite."

Sophie's eyes widened in shock. "Oh, no. As long as we can fit a double bed, the room is perfect. I never did cotton to those king-size beds. We might as well sleep in separate rooms."

"Which explains why we have three kids in as many years," Alex drawled close to her ear.

She stepped on his foot. "Oh, look, Norman. This room is perfect for little Becky."

Alex tightened his fingers around her forearm and led her away before she gave the real-estate agent their entire nonexistent life history. Her ability to lie convincingly at will was a source of concern. Could he believe that everything she'd told him the past couple of days was the complete truth?

They finished the tour just as another couple pulled up the driveway. Melinda looked torn between the new arrivals and the prospect of losing a potential sale.

"We'll wander about the grounds by ourselves. Norman might need a bit of convincing." Sophie winked. "You know, you can take the boy out of the city, but you can't take the city out of the boy."

Melinda nodded. "Okay, well, I'll be here if you have any questions."

"Sure thing," Sophie said. She took Alex's hand and pulled him outside.

He exhaled in relief. "Well, now, *Mindy Sue*. What have you got to say for yourself?"

She fluttered her eyelashes. "Why, Norman, I do declare you seem a bit perturbed."

Alex hooked his arm through hers and began to meander toward the truck. "You're a little too good at this. Do you do it often?"

"This is nothing. You should see me when I crash weddings."

He lowered his head and groaned. The woman needed a keeper. "Do you really?"

She laughed and playfully punched his shoulder.

"Not since I turned eighteen. Lighten up. No one was hurt by the pretense. We didn't take her away from a customer."

"And that makes it all right?"

The light in her eyes dimmed. "I'm sorry. I really didn't think you'd mind. I was just having some fun."

Was he overreacting? After all, he had played right along with her. He could just as easily have laughed when Sophie made her introduction and given his real name to the agent.

He opened the door for her. "Can we go now?"

She slipped into the seat and glanced up at him. "Let's get you back home and put you to bed with a nice hot water bottle. You've had enough excitement for one day."

"Is that your roundabout way of saying I'm boring?"

"That's not a word I would use to describe you." Her full lips curved upward. "On second thought, let's skip the hot water bottle and just put you to bed. Maybe you need a little more excitement in your life."

Alex chuckled. She could be so damned infuriating and then she would turn around and say something that made it impossible to stay angry with her. "What am I going to do with you?"

What am I going to do without you? That question bothered him even more.

He closed the door and walked around the vehicle to the driver's side. As he reached for the handle, he took one last look at the farm. With the split-rail fence and acres of undeveloped land, he could understand the appeal for Sophie. Open spaces. No walls. The opposite of everything she believed his world to be. He didn't have much time left to convince her otherwise. Her vacation was nearly over.

Eight

Alex stopped by the study to make a quick check of his E-mail, but not quick enough for Sophie's liking. She gave him five minutes of peace before she turned on her cassette player and began dancing around the room. Her sultry movements made concentration impossible. She twirled her way over to the desk and arched her back until her hair spilled over the keyboard.

"I thought you were on vacation," she whispered. As she stood upright again, he grasped the fabric of her skirt and tugged her onto his lap.

"What's that piece of music called?"

She lowered the volume a notch and snuggled closer. *"Scheherazade."*

"The lady who told all those *Arabian Nights* tales. Was she a friend of yours in a past life?"

"You figured me out."

Her hair brushed against his cheek and warm breath tickled his neck. "So, tell me, my little tale-teller, what are you going to do after you leave here?"

"In general?"

Alex nodded.

"I have a few jobs to complete and a couple more in the works."

"And if they don't pan out?"

Her shoulders rolled in a casual shrug. "Something will come up. It always does. I know how to take care of myself."

"Did I imply that you couldn't?"

She shook her head slowly.

He stroked his hand over her shoulder until she purred with contentment. "Your work. You could do it from anywhere, right?"

"I suppose. But it's hard to strap my computer and printer on my back and take it on the road."

"That's not what I meant."

"I know." She slid her arms around his back and began to massage the tight muscles at the base of his neck. She wiggled in his lap. "You're too serious. Loosen up a little."

Alex recognized a diversionary tactic when he saw one. Was she trying to avoid a conversation about their future because she knew what he wanted to ask, or because she didn't know? He wasn't ready to find out.

"I can't change a lifetime of habit without some skilled help. Do you know anyone who could take on the job?"

"Oh, I suppose I could find some time here and there to give you a few private lessons."

He unhooked the small cassette player from her waist and placed it on the desk. "How soon could you begin?"

She turned and straddled her legs across his thighs. "There's no time like the present."

He shot a quick glance toward the door. "Anyone could walk in."

"Lesson number one. Experiences are infinitely more exciting if there's an element of danger involved. In this case, the danger of getting caught by the staff. Now let me see." She nipped at his earlobe. "Where do I start when there's so much to be done?"

Her fingers walked a delicate path down his chest to his belt buckle. The full swirls of her kelly green skirt hampered her efforts to find his zipper. With one swift yank she managed to tug the elastic waist garment right over her head and dropped it on the floor. Her peasant-style blouse followed in a similar hasty fashion.

When he caught the scent of apricot, he knew he was done for. His body tensed and turned rock hard in seconds. "You call this loosening up?"

A hint of mischief glinted in her eyes. "I know the exercises can be grueling, but I guarantee the results will be worth the effort."

He buried his head between her full round breasts, tasting the sweetness. Her sharp intake of breath, the moans and sighs that escaped her lips, blended with the gentle strains of violin music. She nuzzled closer, tormenting him with her slow, twisting movements.

He lifted her onto the desk and eased her lace panties off. His jeans followed suit.

"You're a quick learner," she muttered. She

wrapped her legs around his waist and drew him closer.

He felt her damp heat pressing against him. Her short panting breaths conveyed her desire and her impatience. She gripped the desk and arched up as he entered her. Her eyes glazed over and she let out a satisfied moan.

''Nice,'' she said in a husky whisper.

''Better than nice,'' he added. She was the closest thing to heaven to be found on this earth.

They moved together as one, attuned to every nuance·of the other's body. The rhythm built quickly; control slipped away. All his questions, his reservations faded to the recesses of his mind. Making love to her was a feast for the senses. She satisfied a hunger he hadn't known he possessed.

Her hands explored, her tongue tasted and her gaze remained fixed on his. She knew what she did to him and she enjoyed watching the way he reacted to her. Every time was different, but always fevered and intense. She lived for the moment and made each moment count.

When she climaxed, his name was on her lips. She locked her arms around his neck in a vise grip as if she were afraid he might try to leave. Right now, sheltered tightly in his embrace and trembling, she was his in every sense of the word.

But for how long?

After their breathing returned to normal, after the last shudder faded and she smiled up at him as if he was the only man in the world, the question still haunted him.

After dinner Sophie joined Alex for a ride around the property. He had been relatively quiet during the evening meal and even less talkative now. She knew she was responsible for his mood, since she had cut him off every time he tried to talk about anything remotely serious. What was she afraid of? Obviously he wanted to make some kind of future plans; otherwise, he would have told her to take a hike already. Wasn't that what she wanted?

A red sky flamed overhead. The steady clap of hooves made an eerie echo off the walls. She leaned forward and stroked the horse's neck, finding comfort in the gesture. The Sanctuary might be a fortress, but she didn't find a sense of safety in the sheltered estate. She felt edgy and anxious, as if something was about to happen.

She turned to find Alex watching her with a curious expression.

"What are you doing?" he asked.

"Just studying the walls. The big, thick walls." She slid off Elvis's back and wrapped the reins around a wooden bench.

He dismounted. "They're imposing, I guess, but for a few days at a time, it's not so bad."

Her gaze traveled over the vast landscape then back to him. "You don't sound overly attached to the place."

"I'm not." He raised one boot-clad foot to the seat of the bench and sat on the back. She rested her hand on his thigh.

"So why drive yourself into an early heart attack trying to keep the place up?"

"What would you suggest?"

"Did you ever consider selling it?"

His fingers clenched the wooden slat. "Oh. Been talking to Damon?"

A stab of guilt turned her insides. "He mentioned how difficult it is to keep up an estate this size when neither of you actually live here."

He folded his arms across his broad chest. "And what else has my oh-so-concerned brother been telling you?"

Sophie recoiled from his bitter words. The chasm between the two brothers was too deep to be bridged by her. Why had she thought to try? She couldn't explain herself. While Alex adopted this defensive attitude, he would misinterpret her motives. "Nothing. Forget I said anything."

"No. I'd be interested to hear."

"Look, apparently I was mistaken."

"About what?"

"Your shared past. I understood that he felt guilty about…" She inhaled a deep breath. This was not a subject she wanted to get into with him.

"My ex-fiancée?" he finished for her.

"Well, yes," she spilled out.

His dark eyes narrowed into angry slits. "What exactly did he tell you?"

She shook her head and took a step back. "Can we drop this?"

"No." He caught her wrist as she tried to turn away.

"All right. He told me he'd had an affair with your ex. He's felt bad that it caused this rift between the two of you. He even brought me here as his fiancée, hoping that you and I would hit it off and then the score would be even. Of course, when I discovered his intent, I told him I wouldn't play along."

''That's big of you.'' Sarcasm resonated in his voice.

Squaring her shoulders, she met his suspicious gaze. ''Excuse me?''

''While Damon was baring his soul to you, did he also happen to mention that he'd been involved with Marie before she became 'engaged' to me? Or that he'd promised her a big chunk of money if she got me to the altar.''

''No,'' she said quietly. A shudder ran through her. ''And I'll bet he never mentioned that he thinks you bear more than a passing resemblance to her, either. He probably chose you for that reason.''

No doubt, she thought. Had Alex chosen her for that reason, too? Had he made love to her while thinking of his ex-fiancée? A wave of nausea washed over her.

''If one of us gets married, the estate will be sold and the rather substantial trust that supports the bills will be divided. So, you see, I'm not exactly working myself into a heart attack trying to keep the place up.''

She shook her head. Damon had played her for a fool again and she had fallen for his I-know-I'm-no-good-but-I-feel-so-bad routine right down the line. Obviously she'd been set up. But why? ''He left that part out.''

''You mean he didn't offer you a similar deal if you could find a way to get me to sell?''

Her stomach clenched painfully as if she'd been sucker punched. ''You think I slept with you for money?''

''I didn't say that.''

''You didn't have to.'' Her choked words were barely a whisper. A gnawing pain ate at her insides.

''You already admitted that he offered you money to act as his fiancée.''

''A donation to charity. There is a difference.''

''Put yourself in my place and tell me what you'd think.''

I would believe in you, believe in what we shared together. Obviously to him, they hadn't shared anything more than sex. ''I can't. I trust what I feel. You trust what you've already decided to be the truth.''

''You and Damon lied to me from the beginning and I'm wrong?''

''I didn't say you were wrong. You have every right to keep your home if that's what you want. But I can't help wonder why you hold on to a place you don't particularly like unless you see it as a way to control your family.''

''I'm sure that's what Damon told you.''

''No, Alex. Believe it or not, I figured that out all by myself.'' An emptiness settled over her heart. She wiped her palms along her pant legs and rolled her shoulders to relieve the tension. The start of a headache pricked at her temples.

Why was she surprised? For a while she'd deluded herself into thinking Alex wanted a relationship, but she couldn't blame him for her fantasies. Eventually all men looked for a way out, an excuse to end the affair. She need look no further than her own history to know that. Her father hadn't even stayed around to see the birth of his daughter.

How odd. She never realized how much that affected her, yet it had impacted every relationship she'd had as an adult. The only difference with Alex was that she hadn't been smart enough to leave before she fell in love. "Oh, well."

"Is that all you have to say?"

"Why should I try to defend myself? You've already made up your mind that I was somehow involved in Damon's plan before we ever slept together. You never trusted me." Her voice trembled with fury.

"I trusted you."

She wished to God that were true, but obviously he'd just been biding his time, waiting for her to say something to prove what he believed all along. "No, you didn't. My relationship with Damon was the last thing you asked about before we made love yesterday, the first thing you asked about afterward, and the first subject you brought up this morning. It doesn't take a psychic to figure out just how little trust you place in me."

"Now, wait a minute." Alex sucked in a large gulp of air and tried to regain control. He was the one being manipulated and used. How had she turned the tables and made him feel guilty?

Sophie untied Elvis's reins and, using the bench for leverage, pulled herself onto the horse.

"Where are you going?" he asked.

"Back to the house." She made a clicking sound with her teeth and turned Elvis in the direction of the stable.

Alex stared at her retreating back. He kicked the wall and let out a grunt. Was Sophie right? Did he hold on to the house to keep control of Damon and Elaine? He told himself he was acting in their best interest, but they obviously knew how to look out for themselves. They didn't need him. Elaine would find herself another rich sucker when her money ran out, and his brother…

Brother? That was the biggest joke of all. Damon had never thought of Alex as a brother. In fact, Damon had never wanted any part of the Sinclair family, right down to refusing his stepfather's request to adopt him.

Alex put his foot in the stirrup and pulled himself up onto Windancer. Maybe it was time to accept that he didn't have a family. So, why the hell did he need a family home?

Sophie threw her clothes into the canvas suitcase with total disregard. Although she'd had time to calm down, she still believed that leaving was the wisest decision. In truth, she had no one to blame but herself. No good came from telling lies. Damon had manipulated her because she had allowed him to.

Right now she was furious with Damon, but Alex's accusations cut to her very soul. If he believed she would sleep with him for money, then he didn't think much of her anyway. Why bother trying to convince him otherwise?

She checked her watch. Her taxi would be outside the gate in another five minutes and she wanted to be waiting before the driver tried to enter the estate. She jotted a "thanks for your hospitality" note and left it next to the phone. After one last check of the closet, she flipped the clasps on the suitcase and lifted it off the bed.

As she started down the hall, she heard the sound of approaching footsteps. Swallowing the lump in her throat, she turned abruptly.

"Soph?" Damon arched his eyebrow quizzically.
"What are you doing?"

"I would have thought that was obvious."

He grabbed hold of her suitcase and set it on the
floor. "Did you and Alex have a fight?" He sounded
genuinely concerned, but that only proved he could
lie at will. Had she ever misread him! Then again,
she hadn't been able to read Alex, either. There was
a lesson to be learned here. Obviously this was a
family with a lot to hide.

She inhaled deeply and counted to ten. The urge
to strike her palm across his arrogant face was almost
more than she could fight. "I'm not sure what your
game is, but my part in it is over."

"I told you—"

"You told me, all right," she snapped bitterly. "A
string of lies designed to push all the right buttons—
his and mine. You couldn't care less about making
amends with your brother."

"What's he been telling you?"

"He told me the parts of the story you left out,
friend. Particularly why you're so interested in having him sell this place."

Damon's jaw tightened and his eyes turned as cold
as blue ice. "Did he also mention how he rides
roughshod over our lives like a third-world dictator?
We need his permission to touch our trust fund, his
cosignature to take a loan."

Her hands trembled with anger. "Maybe your
stepfather knew what he was doing when he set up
the trust. You're a thirty-year-old man, and a gutless
wonder at that. You can't stand up to Alex yourself
so you set me up to do your dirty work. Well, you

figured him wrong. And you highly overrated my usefulness as well.''

Damon grinned as if he knew some juicy secret. ''I don't think so.''

''He wasn't fooled. He just played along until he learned what you were up to.'' She settled her purse on her shoulder and lifted her suitcase. ''Get a job, Damon. He's not selling the house.''

''How are you getting home?''

''Don't worry.'' She let out a laugh. ''Never mind. I forgot who I was talking to.'' She felt the tears welling in her eyes, but she refused to cry in front of him.

''You're in love with him. I never thought I'd live to see the day.''

Steeling herself against the painful emotions, she raised her chin. ''Still looking for something you can exploit? He thinks I'm in on your twisted little plot and it will be a cold day in hell before he lets you win.''

''Don't be too sure.''

''Oh, I am. And I'm leaving here before I do any more damage.''

He touched her arm, and she swatted his hand away like an annoying fly.

''I'm sorry, Sophie. I really like you.''

She would hate to see what Damon was capable of if he didn't like her. ''You're not sorry. You're a cynical bastard and you only care about yourself.''

''You try growing up the poor relative of the rich kid, and you'd become cynical, too.''

''Oh, you're breaking my heart,'' she wailed dramatically. ''Hell, it's not just the money for you. You are so consumed with jealousy that you'd do anything to hurt him, even at the expense of your friends.

Why don't you just try growing up, period. He's your *step*brother, as you so often point out. He doesn't owe you a damn thing." She strode to the steps and turned back. "Enjoy your life at The Sanctuary. If ever a person was suited to the place, it's you. You're as cold and hard as the stone facade."

Sophie held her breath until she cleared the front door. Thankful she was a light packer, she ran with her canvas bag down the winding driveway to the gate. She leaned against the outside wall just beneath a spotlight, waiting with dread for her cab. The minutes ticked off slowly, but finally she saw a set of headlights and shortly thereafter the white taxi pulled up to the curb.

Alex heard his stepmother's high-pitched commands to the staff and groaned. It figured this would be the only night she and Damon returned before midnight. The day couldn't get any worse, he thought. Leaning his elbows on the desktop, he rested his head in his hands.

Had he been wrong about Sophie? He'd challenged her to teach him how to loosen up. His stepfamily caused him more stress than anything else in his life. The obvious answer to the problem was exactly what she had recommended. Sell the place and let them fend for themselves. Why had he blown a fuse at her suggestion?

The thud of heavy footsteps headed toward the study. Damon lumbered inside, grinning maliciously. "Hey, bro."

"What do you want?"

"You blew it with Sophie." Damon lowered himself into a chair with casual ease. Insolence oozed from every pore.

Alex glared at him contemptuously. "Wasn't that part of the plan?"

"Not exactly."

"Do you think I'd believe anything you tell me?" Damon shrugged. "Probably not."

Alex eyed his stepbrother. Damon looked awfully pleased for someone whose plan had just backfired. "Then what did you hope to gain?"

"I wanted you to know what it's like to have someone manipulating your life." His stone-cold eyes narrowed. "You saw what you wanted to see, Alex. You were so ready to believe she was involved with me that you let your suspicions cloud what was right in front of your face."

"And what was that?"

"A woman who loved you. She had no idea what I was doing. And while I'll admit I figured you'd be the one who fell, not her, I can't say I'm unhappy with the results. You hurt her badly and I know how that goes against your high-and-mighty principles."

"Looking out for the financial affairs of the family is hardly comparable to a deliberate plan to screw up my life. When are you going to stop?"

"I think you already know the answer to that."

Alex rose to his feet. He balled his fingers into fists. "Doesn't it bother you that you used a friend to get to me?"

Damon shook his head. "You used her, too. The only difference is, I didn't sleep with her to get information."

"Neither did I." Alex felt the anger rising. No doubt his stepbrother had made sure Sophie believed he had. He needed to talk to her, to explain.

"Then, I suppose you're in love with her."

Alex walked to the window and gazed out into the night sky. "That's none of your business."

"It is if you ever want to see her again."

"Meaning?"

"She left. Packed her bag and called a cab over an hour ago."

Alex turned slowly. Fury built to blind rage. "You let her leave by herself at night!"

"*Let her?* I have no more control over her than you do. She does what she wants. And she wanted to leave before you started blaming her for all my maneuvering."

"Where did she go?"

Damon slouched in the chair and smiled. "You want to find her? What are you offering in return?"

Alex crossed the room and stood next to the leather chair, towering over Damon. "Do you think I'm going to let you blackmail me? I'll find her on my own."

Damon recoiled slightly but raised his head in cold defiance. "You'll never find her without me. She doesn't have a lease, no credit cards, no cable TV bills, only a post office box in the central post office of New York and an answering service for business calls. The woman does not have a traceable paper trail." He rubbed his hands together. "Like it or not, you have to deal with me."

Alex swallowed a groan. This time Damon had gone too far—playing with people's lives as if they were pieces on a chessboard. Although Alex had already made a decision to sell the estate, he refused to give his stepbrother the satisfaction of telling him now. "No, I don't. There is somebody who will be able to find her."

"Who?"

"Now, do you think I'd tell you?" He turned and strode across the room, pausing at the door. "I want you out of here by the time I get back."

"Now that's one thing you have no say over unless you've decided to sell the place."

"True." Alex nodded and cracked a hint of a smile. "But keep in mind, I could just as easily sell the estate to a charity for one dollar. That would take a huge chunk out of the money you were hoping to gain."

He walked out of the room, leaving Damon with his jaw hanging open. In the corridor Alex bumped into his stepmother who'd apparently been hovering outside the door, eavesdropping. Her face blushed furiously.

"I'll be leaving in the morning, Elaine. Tell Cook not to bother with my breakfast."

She wasn't a woman who took orders gracefully. The corner of her mouth twitched angrily, but she inhaled and kept her temper in check. "Where can you be reached in case of an emergency?"

Nice try, he thought. "Call the office. They'll have me paged."

Finding Sophie might prove to be the easy part. Convincing her to hear him out was another matter. Damon was right on one point. Alex had seen what he'd wanted to in Sophie. He'd been so damned adamant about keeping control over his emotions that he'd lost control over his life. In the end, he might well have blown any chance of a relationship with her, but he owed her an apology—and the right to tell him where to go to his face.

Nine

Sophie strolled along the midway, eating a puff of cotton candy. After thirty-six long and lonely hours on several buses, she welcomed the chance to stretch her legs. She waved to Cecille, the woman who ran the ticket booth. Eighty years old and still in control of her faculties, she was an inspiration. The Ferris wheel behind the kiosk twirled in a blur of red-and-blue lights.

Squealing children dragged their parents by the hand, eager to explore the games and rides that made the county fair a yearly ritual for many rural families. Although Sophie had arrived an hour earlier, she hadn't been to see her mother yet. The line for The Amazing Nadia's Tarot Reading was fifteen people deep, more than half of them men hoping for a chance to flirt with the beautiful and exotic Gypsy.

At forty-two, her mother could still turn the head of any male past adolescence.

She had hoped that the games of chance, the side shows and the general excitement of the crowd would afford her a brief escape from the numbing pain that had settled over her heart. No matter how hard she tried to suppress them, her thoughts invariably returned to Alex. How could he even *think* she had seduced him for money? Grudgingly, she admitted that he'd had some help from his stepbrother.

She would get over Damon's betrayal although she would never forgive him. But Alex? What she'd given to him, she'd given freely and despite her instincts, which turned out to be right after all. If any of what they shared had meant a damn thing to him, he would have seen that she loved him.

She sighed. Didn't it just figure that the first time she decided to trust her heart to a man, he couldn't trust his to her?

Around ten-thirty, she finally made her way to her mother's tent. She pushed back the lace tablecloth that hung across the opening. The scent of jasmine incense hung in the air.

"It's about time you wandered in," her mother said without turning.

"You had a busy night. I didn't want to keep you from the paying customers."

"And you think I wouldn't make time for my baby when her heart is broken?" Natalie turned with a dramatic flourish and glided across the canvas floor. She cupped Sophie's face and kissed both cheeks. "How many times have I told you not to fall in love with them? When will you listen to your mama?"

Sophie shrugged casually. "Who says I fell in love?"

"You do. I've felt this sadness for the past day and a half and I knew it had something to do with you."

Sophie knew a denial wouldn't fool either of them. Yes, she had fallen in love. What did she get for her trouble? An emotional kick in the head. "I have no one to blame but myself."

"You're too trusting, honey. I never liked Damon, since the first time I met him."

Once again her mother's insight marveled her. "How did you know he's involved?"

Natalie slipped an arm around her daughter's waist and led her to the worn love seat in the corner of the tent. "Even if I didn't possess this gift, I would know. You told me you were going to meet his family. Which, I warned you at the time, was a bad idea."

Sophie flopped into the seat. "Yeah, well, I didn't listen and now it's too late."

"You can't trust a *gadjo* man. He'll only try to put you in a cage. They don't understand our ways."

"Your ways, Mama. They're not mine. Traveling around the country is fun for a while, but not as a way of life. Not for me."

"Then what's the problem?"

She explained the complicated story—Damon's manipulation, Alex's distrust and even her own responsibility for going to The Sanctuary under false pretenses. Natalie listened, sighing dramatically when Sophie finished. "I would like to feed that rat Damon to one of Ursulla's boa constrictors."

Sophie giggled.

Natalie stroked her daughter's hair. "See, you can still laugh. Everything will be all right. A few weeks with your mama and—"

"I can't stay. I have to head back this weekend." Despite the comfort of her mother's arms, Sophie felt empty, as if a part of her was missing. She closed her eyes and an odd sensation washed over her. That same tingling feeling that blanketed her whenever Alex was near. She shook her head. She must be losing her mind.

"What's wrong?" Natalie asked.

"Nothing."

"I know that look, baby. You're…" She brushed back a hair from Sophie's cheek. "Oh, no, Sophie. You're pregnant."

"Can't be," she returned with certainty.

Natalie arched an eyebrow. "Can't? You and Alex never…"

"Mom!" Sophie grumbled in embarrassment.

"I'm your mother. Do you think I don't know when my child is with child?"

"I was careful."

Natalie waved her hand in a theatrical sweep. "So was I, and I'm having this conversation with my daughter. Think about that."

"This time your impressions are wrong."

"Maybe," she muttered, sounding unconvinced.

Sophie didn't want to consider that her mother could be right, but why else would she feel Alex's presence so strongly when he was a thousand miles away? Could it be his baby, a part of him, that gave her these sensations? What would she do if she was pregnant with Alex's child?

"I'm beat. It's been a long trip."

"You can rest in my trailer. I have a date with a sheriff in a few minutes, but I can cancel if you want me to stay with you."

She smiled bravely. "No. I'll probably hang out with some of the others. You never could resist a man in uniform."

"Are you sure you'll be all right?"

Sophie nodded and pushed to her feet. On the way to her mother's trailer, she stopped for a ride on the Ferris wheel. As a child, she would spend hours on the ride, daydreaming or hiding out when she wanted to be alone.

A summer breeze cooled her warm skin. From the top, the cars along the interstate looked like a stream of shooting stars. She stretched out sideways in the swinging seat and folded her hands over her stomach. Tears flowed freely down her cheeks. She didn't want to feel, to hurt, but she didn't know how to stop the pain. Would she pay for her one white lie the rest of her life?

Alex walked down the nearly deserted thoroughfare of the carnival. An elderly man collected the discarded wrappers that had been tossed carelessly on the ground. Since landing in Kansas City, Alex had spent the past five hours driving through rural towns to find the fairground, after spending half the day trying to track down the location of the Vitabel Traveling Carnival.

He had flown a thousand miles to find an address that was probably less than fifty miles from his apartment. Sophie's mother would know where she lived. At least, that was what he was banking on. What he would say to Sophie when he finally did find her, he hadn't figured out yet.

With luck, The Amazing Nadia would still be around. The carnival was closed for the night and wouldn't open again until noon tomorrow. He didn't look forward to twelve hours in a rented car. A light shone from the tent at the end of the midway and he heard the clink of glasses. With a deep breath, he stepped inside. His jaw dropped and the air caught in his throat. He shook his head and focused again. The slender woman standing with her back to him had the same long mane of ringlets as Sophie but several shades lighter. A brightly colored skirt fell to her ankles and a scarlet red scarf was knotted at her narrow waist.

"I'm closed for the night," she said, and then turned. Vivid green eyes widened and a smile played across her face. "Of course, I could make an exception in your case."

Sophie hadn't exaggerated. Natalie could pass for her sister. And, like her daughter, she was a consummate flirt.

"I need your help finding someone," he said.

"Have a seat." He started to say something, but she cut him off with a wave. "No. Don't tell me anything. I like to get a blind impression first. It helps."

"I'm sure you know already—"

She placed a finger to his lips. "Indulge me."

Alex decided not to antagonize the woman. If she had already spoken to her daughter, she might not want to give him the information he needed. He sat in the folding chair while Natalie took the seat on the opposite side of the table.

She took his hand, closing her warm fingers over his palm. "You seek a woman. A special woman. Right?"

"Yes." It could have been a lucky guess, he thought.

She studied his palm, tracing the lines with a light touch. Her eyebrows arched quizzically. She brought his hand closer and probed one spot as if trying to brush something away. "Very strange."

"What is?" he asked.

Her gaze met his, her eyes narrowed. She studied him intently, then releasing her grip on him, she rose from the table. Her flirtatious smile was gone, replaced by a serious frown.

"You've traveled a long way. A journey motivated by guilt."

That could not have been a lucky guess although she wasn't completely accurate, either. "Not entirely."

Natalie stepped away from the table and perched herself on the edge of a large black trunk.

"Is that all?" Alex asked.

"I don't need anymore." She pushed her hair off her shoulder. In the glow of the muted lighting, her features took on an unmistakable sadness. "You're looking for Sophie. Am I right...Alex?"

His jaw dropped open. Obviously Sophie had spoken to her mother, but that still didn't explain how Natalie knew who he was. "Yes, but how—"

"The crossroad on your life line. My daughter has the same one."

"She said you were good," he said with a tip of his head.

"But you doubted her." Her comment was more

an indictment on the way he'd treated Sophie than his lack of faith in psychic abilities. "I should warn you, you won't receive a warm welcome."

"Her words, or your impression?"

She let out a rich laugh. "Both. She told me what happened. Your mistake was in trusting your head instead of your heart."

"I know my mistake and I plan to rectify it."

Natalie paced the floor, her full skirt swirling as she turned. "You think it will be that easy? Gypsies love passionately and carry a grudge even more passionately. We are not a particularly forgiving lot."

"I just want to talk to her. Could you give me her address?"

Natalie paused as if weighing the decision to answer. He understood her maternal misgivings, but he wasn't going to give up on the only lead he had. Except for Damon, Alex thought bitterly.

"I'll give you the address, but it wouldn't do you much good right now since she's staying with me for the next few days."

He leaned back in the chair. She was here. Relief and anxiety caused his stomach to clench. He thought he'd have another day to figure out what to say to her. However, he wasn't about to wait while he knew where to find her. With Sophie's uncanny ability to sense his presence, she might leave before tomorrow.

"Where is she now?"

"She's either at my trailer at the north end of the park or with some friends behind the main tent. They like to wind down after the townies go home for the night."

"Are you heading there?"

"No. I have a date."

He rose and offered his hand. "Thank you for your help."

Natalie gave him a curious half smile. "I didn't help you, Alex. You seemed to know how to find her on your own."

Sophie tapped a tambourine against her hip and swayed to the hypnotic guitar music. The Romany lullaby was one of her most distinct childhood memories. The bonfire crackled, sending sparks into the air. She backed away from the heat and handed the tambourine to Ursulla. Despite her need to be around friends, she couldn't enjoy the party. The long bus trip had taken a toll and her overwrought emotions weren't helping.

A long shower and a firm mattress sounded heavenly, and not necessarily in that order. She waved her goodbyes and turned away from the gathering. A full moon illuminated the dirt road that led to the row of trailers. Up ahead, she saw the silhouette of a man. Damn. Her mother's date was probably looking for her.

As she got closer, she noticed the scent of Obsession. She froze. Why was she surprised? She had felt his presence for the past hour. Absently, she ran her hand over her stomach. She should feel relieved, but instead she only felt more empty. "What are you doing here?"

"Hello, Sophie." Alex stepped out of the shadows and into the light of an electric lantern. He slipped his hands into the pockets of his cotton Dockers and shrugged his shoulders like a little boy about to be punished. And he should be, she thought.

"Look, I'm really tired."

"We need to talk."

"Why? Didn't you say enough the last time we talked?"

"I owe you an apology."

She walked past him without meeting his gaze. Her emotions were too raw to deal with him in a logical and rational manner. Who was she kidding? Nothing about her relationship with Alex had been logical since day one. "How did you find me?"

"I had a friend track down the carnival."

"Well, thanks for the visit," she grumbled. "Forgive me if I don't stay and chat."

"I said I was sorry."

She let out a bitter laugh. "No. Like a typical male, you said you *owed* me an apology, but you didn't offer one. Well, I don't want to collect it. I'm going to sleep."

Thankfully, he didn't argue. She was in no mood to listen to his guilty excuses. As she stepped up onto the wooden platform, she heard a squeak behind her. She turned slowly. Alex had stretched out in an aluminum chaise longue.

"What are you doing?"

"I have to sleep somewhere. This is as good a place as any."

"You'll get eaten alive by mosquitoes. Why don't you go back to The Sanctuary?"

He shot her a determined smile. "Not until we've talked."

If he thought he could use emotional blackmail on her, he was sadly mistaken. "Fine. Enjoy the night."

She stormed inside and dropped into a vinyl easy chair. Rasputin, her mother's feline companion, glanced up at her from his position on the sofa. After a disinterested glance, he yawned and put his head back down. If only she could relax.

What did Alex want? She refused to believe that any sense of remorse had led him here. That would require that he hold feelings for her.

The rumble of distant thunder rattled the window-panes. Alex began whistling "Singing in the Rain" in a loud pitch. She would not give in. She would not feel guilty. If he got wet, that was his problem.

She rested her head back and closed her eyes. Raindrops tapped against the roof. With a groan of resignation, she vaulted from the chair. She couldn't let him sleep in the rain, even though she believed he deserved a good soaking.

When she opened the door, Alex was standing on the top step, sheltered by a canvas awning. She exhaled deeply. "Come on. You can sleep on the couch."

"Are you sure your mother won't mind?" he asked.

As if he cared, since he obviously knew she would let him in.

"I'm sure she read it in her tarot cards."

Sophie glanced at the starry sky and realized the few scattered raindrops weren't going to amount to anything. She should have waited another minute before giving in.

"Thank you," he said as he brushed past before she could change her mind.

A tingle ran through her. She folded her arms over her chest to hide the physical reaction of her traitorous body. "The couch is lumpy and one of the springs is loose."

"Sounds cozy."

"You won't think so when Rasputin hisses at you all night. It's his bed."

"I take it Rasputin is a cat?"

She laughed. "A harmless little kitty."

Alex skirted his way around a mounted table and ducked under a wall cabinet before stepping into the living room area. The trailer utilized every inch of its compact space.

"I'll be right back," Sophie mumbled, and disappeared behind a lacy curtain.

As he lowered himself onto the sofa, what he thought was a leopard-print pillow moved. The cat arched its back and emitted a guttural groan. *A harmless little kitty?* Rasputin, a full-grown ocelot, didn't take kindly to being uprooted. He perched himself on the arm and glared at Alex with his golden eyes.

"Look, boy, I can't do anything about this arrangement. Complain to Sophie."

She reemerged from behind the curtain and dropped a pillow and blanket in his lap. "If you don't like the accommodations, leave."

"I'm not complaining. Rasputin is."

"He can sleep with me." She lifted the spotted cat into her arms and stroked her long fingers over his head.

"Lucky kitty," he muttered under his breath. "Watch out for the claws."

Her emerald eyes locked on his. "I trust him not to hurt me." She turned and left the room.

Her deeper meaning wasn't lost on him. She didn't trust him anymore. He couldn't really blame her. He considered himself lucky that she had allowed him inside.

He sprawled across the sofa and got jabbed by the

loose spring she had warned him about. After several attempts, he found a semicomfortable position, but sleep eluded him.

Although less than ten feet and one sheer curtain separated them, Sophie had erected an emotional wall that seemed impenetrable. Or was it? She could just as easily have let him sleep outside. Perhaps Sophie wasn't quite as angry as she wanted him to believe.

Ten

Alex peered through half-closed eyes to the kitchen area. Sophie stood at the sink, filling a teakettle. A pair of cutoff shorts hugged her round bottom and a white shirt was knotted at the waist. Her damp hair sprung into curls across her back.

"Good morning," he called out.

She grunted a response. The night hadn't improved her mood.

He stretched his cramped muscles and sat up. "What are you up to?"

Silence answered him. She pulled two mugs from a cabinet along with a jar of instant coffee. As she showered her undivided attention on the pot of water, she did her best to ignore his presence.

He joined her in the kitchen, standing deliberately close. The scent of apricot brought back memories that made him grow hard with desire. "You can't ignore me forever," he muttered in her ear.

She took a step back. "Wanna bet?"

"You answered me."

She smacked a spoon down on the counter. "I can't deal with this right now."

"Then don't. I'll take you to breakfast."

"You're the one I can't deal with." She turned to face him. "Why are you here?"

"I needed to clear up a few things. I had an interesting talk with Damon...."

She cut him off with a wave. "I don't want to discuss your brother."

"He's not my brother."

A muffled gasp escaped from her parted lips. She leaned against the linoleum counter, her gaze lowered in sadness. "I'm sorry."

Her sorrow puzzled him. That she cared after what Damon and he had put her through was a testament to her compassionate character. "Why?"

"Because he was your brother before you met me."

He brushed his fingers over her clenched jaw and left his hand resting against her cheek. "No. Not in his eyes."

"He's jealous."

"It goes beyond that. He resents the hell out of me."

"That's his problem, not yours."

"Obviously not." He shook his head. "I knew what he was capable of and I let him manipulate me anyway."

Her sympathies seemed to vanish and her earlier anger returned. She pushed his hand away. "You wanted to believe the worst about me. I can't fight against that.''

Alex tried to reach for her, but she ducked under his arm. ''Are you being completely fair, Sophie?''

Fire flickered in her eyes. ''Oh, don't let me forget that I was the one who lied in the first place. The difference is, I never tried to hurt you.''

''That's not what I meant.'' He grunted in frustration. ''You were taken in by Damon, too. Weren't you?''

''Only to the extent that I wanted to be.''

He cocked his eyebrow in question. ''And why did you want to be?''

She looked away. ''It doesn't matter.''

''I think it does.''

Sophie shrugged indifferently. How could she explain what she didn't understand herself? The first time she caught Damon in a lie she should have known he would do it again. She chose to believe him anyway because she had wanted an excuse to stay at The Sanctuary. But why, when all the signs pointed to a painful conclusion? ''We all played parts and now the show is over.''

''I don't buy that.''

''Isn't that exactly what you accused me of?''

He leaned forward, pinning her in the corner. ''Before I had all the facts.''

She planted her hands on her hips. ''And what facts are you referring to?''

''That Damon's resentment and greed ran so deep that he would hurt you to get to me.''

She blinked back a tear that threatened to fall. ''He didn't hurt me, Alex. You did.''

"I know. And I want a chance to make it up to you."

"Why? Because I remind you of Marie?"

His face contorted in disgust. "If you reminded me of her, I wouldn't be here."

"Yet you asked her to marry you."

"A mistake."

"Did you love her?" She needed to know. Since Alex had told her of their resemblance, she had been unable to shake the notion that his ex-fiancée was still very much in his heart.

"I liked the idea of having a stable family life again. After my father died, things went out of control. Elaine and Damon were going through their inheritance as if it were unlimited. The family was falling apart. I somehow imagined that my marriage would bring the family back together. After all, she got along so well with Damon, who was going through a bad time." Alex clenched and unclenched his fingers. "I didn't realize how well until I came home from work early one day to find them together."

"What did you do?"

"Actually, I laughed. Marie kept asking Damon if she was still going to get her money while Damon tried to shut her up. It was quite comical." He gazed at her shocked expression. "So, in answer to your earlier question, I guess I didn't love her or I would have felt something. I was more hurt by Damon's actions."

He took a step closer, brushing his arm against her. His woodsy scent surrounded her. Her heart beat a little faster and her nerve endings pricked to attention. Apparently her mind had no control over her body.

"So, what do you say? Can we give this another try?"

"What makes you think I want to see you anymore?" she challenged, trying to muster her anger. His admission didn't change the fact that he hadn't trusted her.

He grinned. "You let me sleep here last night."

A warm flush rose to her face. "I thought it was going to rain."

"You cared if I got wet," he gently accused. He edged slightly closer.

"Did not."

"Then you wanted my company for the night?"

She shot him an angry glare. "Make your point."

"We shared something special."

Her eyes rounded. "Hello. Anybody home? We shared sex. No trust, no commitment, no emotion. There's nothing particularly special about that."

Deep frown lines etched in his forehead. "You don't believe that any more than I do."

She had felt something more, something *special,* but Alex obviously hadn't. His actions proved that. However, she didn't want to debate the issue. She felt confused and conflicted and not at all in a frame of mind to make any decisions about the future of their relationship. "Let's not do this, Alex."

"All I'm asking is for a chance to make it up to you."

"Why bother? We don't even live in the same state."

He dismissed her excuse with a flip of his hand.

"Stamford is an hour from the city. Any other problems?"

"I'm mad as hell at you."

"I know," he said with a slight nod. "And you Gypsies aren't a forgiving lot. Your mother warned me."

"Why didn't you listen?"

He lowered his head until their faces were inches apart. Warm breath fluttered over her neck.

"Because we share a crossroad in our life lines."

She exhaled a sigh and shook her head. "Mama will say anything the paying customers want to hear."

"I didn't pay her."

"Then you better hope she didn't put a curse on your life."

"I've got Damon. Isn't that enough of a curse on my life?"

She laughed even though she didn't want to. The scent of him, the warmth radiating from his solid body just inches from her own, evoked sensations she could neither suppress nor ignore.

"Come on, Sophie. We'll start from scratch. It's our fate."

"I'll think about it," she found herself saying. *Nice, Sophie, that's asserting yourself.* She pressed her palms against his shoulder and pushed him back. She had no willpower when he stood so close to her. And worse, he knew it.

His lips curved upward despite his effort to keep a straight face. "How about this afternoon?"

"I can't. I'm sketching on the midway today." She stepped around him and switched off the fire under the teakettle.

"Tonight?" he asked, backing out of the kitchen area.

She shrugged her shoulders indifferently. "We'll see."

When he reached the front door, he turned back. "I'll pick you up at six."

"I didn't say yes."

"But you will."

His confidence bordered on arrogance. He chuckled and slipped outside at the same second she tossed a spoon at him. Of course he was sure of himself. She had given him no reason to think she had any backbone where he was concerned. What could she reasonably expect to gain by giving him another chance?

What were his expectations? At no time did he mention the words *trust* or *love*. So what did he want from her? If he thought she would hop right back into bed with him, then he would be disappointed. Even if she had to torture herself in the process.

Sophie tossed her sketch pad on the chair and emptied the money from her pockets onto the counter. She rolled her shoulders to relieve the aching. Eight portraits and twenty-two caricatures had made for a busy afternoon. She welcomed the work because it kept her from dwelling on Alex. Not that she had escaped completely. She felt his presence and even caught him watching her a couple of times in the afternoon.

As she started to change for her date, Natalie walked in, surrounded by the jangle of her costume jewelry. She shed her red lace shawl and draped it over the lamp. "Is he here?" she whispered.

Sophie shook her head. "How was your date last night?"

Natalie sighed. "Heavenly. And lucky for you, or I might have come home last night." She picked up the sketch pad and glanced through the pictures.

"Well, you would have stumbled over Alex sleeping on the couch...alone."

"It didn't seem to discourage him. I've noticed he's been hanging around most of the day. You probably wouldn't listen if I told you to steer clear."

Sophie stepped into her black miniskirt and pulled it over her hips. "Then why did you tell him where to find me?"

"Very nice," Natalie mumbled, seemingly distracted. She turned the drawing of Alex's naked form toward Sophie. "What were you saying, dear?"

Sophie moaned and grabbed her sketch pad. "Forget it."

"Be careful, baby. I know you love him, but he's got a very strong personality and he'll try to control you. You'll end up hurting each other."

"Mama, I know what I'm doing."

Natalie patted her daughter's stomach. "I'm not sure you do."

"You're wrong about that."

"If you say so," she said without conviction. "Anyway, I'll be out again tonight."

Sophie arched her eyebrow. "Two nights in a row sounds serious for you. You better be careful yourself."

"We're old friends. I see him every time I pass through this area of the country."

"Interesting. How come you never mentioned him?"

Natalie straightened the collar of Sophie's midriff-baring blouse. "We're not discussing my love life. You're the one who ran off to the 'circus' because your heart was broken."

"I didn't run away. I told you I would be here this week. And didn't you just finish warning me to 'steer clear'?"

Natalie kissed her daughter's cheek. "You're not gonna listen to me anyway."

"I'm just having dinner with him."

"All right, make your own mistakes. I'll be here when you need me again."

Sophie groaned. Her mother hadn't been wrong yet. Was she making the mistake of her life? Too late now, she thought. A knock on the door told her Alex had arrived.

Alex pulled the car into the hotel parking lot. Sophie had been predictably quiet during the fifteen-minute ride. Apparently she wasn't done punishing him. He could start with the outfit she wore. The miniskirt exposed the long, long length of her shapely legs. Her shirt exposed a hint of satiny skin along her flat stomach. The vee neckline gave just a peek of the swells of her breasts. All together, the effect was enough to make him uncomfortable in his jeans.

"What are we doing here?" she asked when he turned off the engine.

"Having dinner."

"In a hotel?" She peered at him from beneath thick dark lashes. Her lips formed a pout that seemed a cross between annoyance and amusement. "If you're hoping for more than food, you're going to walk away hungry.''

"I wanted a place where we could talk in private. Nothing happens unless you say so."

"Don't hold your breath."

He chuckled as he exited the car and walked around to open her door. He had no doubt he could make her eat her words in under an hour if he chose to. She responded too easily and too passionately to his touch. He also knew that the next time they made love, it had to be her idea and on her terms. Sex wasn't enough. He wanted her trust. And more than that, he wanted her heart.

He took hold of her delicate hand and helped her from the car. More than a few heads turned as they walked across the parking lot and through the lobby to the bank of elevators. The scent of her perfume in the close confines wreaked havoc on his hormones. Did he honestly think he would be able to play the perfect gentleman for the entire evening?

Alex poured a glass of champagne and handed it to Sophie. She leaned back in the settee and took a sip. Bubbles tickled her nostrils and the chilled liquid soothed her parched throat. She glanced around the large suite. At least she wouldn't be staring at a king-size bed while eating dinner. Alex and a bed in the same room didn't make her hungry for food.

He sat next to her. The heat from his body enveloped her despite the air-conditioning. Her light-headed feeling had nothing to do with the champagne and everything to do with her companion. Agreeing to dinner in his hotel suite was a bad idea. At this rate she'd be undressing before the food arrived. She pressed her knees together and tugged at the hem of her skirt.

His gaze locked on her. The corner of his mouth twitched in amusement.

"You wanted to talk?" she reminded him.

"Right to the point, huh?"

"We've wasted enough time with games. And, while I'll admit I'm to blame for most of that—"

"Not entirely. And I agree, no more games." He took a large gulp of the champagne and put the flute on the end table. His expression grew serious. "I want you to come to Stamford with me."

She twisted her fingers together in her lap. "I can't take any more vacation time. I have to get back to work."

"I meant I want you to live with me. You're self-employed. You can set up your office in my condo. There's plenty of room."

Her jaw dropped. His offer came as such a shock that she could barely breathe. Admittedly, she had once hoped for a commitment from him, but she had envisioned something more along the lines of a standing Saturday-night date. She hadn't lived with anyone since turning seventeen.

"Phew. Now who's getting right to the point?"

"You wanted straightforward honesty."

"I wanted trust." She fidgeted with her silver bracelet. He covered her hands to still her nervous gesture. "Why?"

"Trust has to be built, and the more time we spend together, the better our chances."

His point was logical, but she wanted an emotional answer. Was his offer motivated by his desire to have her with him or his need to control?

She had never felt about any man the way she felt about Alex. Her anger aside, he had tapped into a part of her she had denied existed. But live with him?

"I'm not a good roommate. I enjoy my independence too much."

"I'm not offering you indentured servitude."

"That's what you say. Next thing I know, you're telling me what to wear, when to come home, who I can see…"

He laughed. "Sophie…"

She chewed her bottom lip. "Don't you believe in starting slow? Go on a few dates? Then we could try taking a trip together, one that involves a car and a road map. If we survive that, then we can think about cohabitating."

"Is that what you want?"

"I don't know." She raked back a handful of hair with an unsteady hand. Had she ever miscalculated! She had prepared for anything he might say—except this. "Where is our dinner?"

"You're changing the subject."

"I can't make a decision like this on an empty stomach." She swatted his hand off her leg. "And I can't make a decision when you're getting me aroused."

"Sorry," he said, sounding anything but contrite.

"You should think about what you're asking."

"I have."

"For how long? Two days ago, I got the impression that you didn't want to see me anymore. And they say women are fickle."

Alex ignored her dig and slid closer. He squeezed his fingers over her thigh. Her determination was crumbling like a stale cookie. A soft sigh escaped. Damn the man and his ability to disarm her!

He had promised nothing would happen without her say so. All she had to do was tell him to stop. Show a little backbone, she chided her conscience. Instead, she leaned into him as he brushed a kiss over her mouth. He tasted like champagne, intoxicating her.

A knock on the door gave her a much-needed distraction. He let out a deep groan as she pulled back.

"Saved," she muttered.

He chuckled. "Did you need saving?"

She inhaled deeply to level her erratic breathing. "Apparently. You're a dangerous man."

"How so?"

Because I love you. Not that she would admit as much. After all, he hadn't offered her anything more than a roof over her head. An arrangement he could terminate whenever the mood struck him, giving him all the control in their relationship. He wasn't just asking her to live with him, he was asking her to trust him without offering the same in return.

"You'd better answer the door. Cold food loses some of its appeal."

Eleven

———

During dinner Sophie picked at her food. Normally Alex wouldn't have given it a thought, but she had never been shy about eating in front of him. He silently cursed himself for making his offer so soon, but patience had never been one of his virtues. How would he proceed if she declined?

An occasional dating relationship was not what he wanted. And Sophie didn't seem ready to make a long-term commitment. Living together seemed like a logical middle ground. Judging by her rare silence, she still had doubts, though.

"Something wrong with the food?" he asked.

"No. I had a couple of hot dogs for lunch and they're sitting like lead right here." She rubbed her hand over her stomach, looking slightly queasy.

"Oh. I thought maybe something else was bothering you."

She placed her napkin on the table and slid her chair back. Despite the early hour, she seemed tired. She rose at the same time as him.

"I guess I should be getting back."

"Why?" The evening wasn't going quite the way he had envisioned.

As he came around the table, she backed herself into the wall.

"Because I can't make a decision this important based on sex."

"Who said anything about sex?"

Her eyebrows arched in confusion. "Then what's the point?"

Did she believe the only thing between them was sex? Or worse, did she think that was all he wanted from her? "You can sleep here."

She giggled nervously. "Like I'll get any sleep with you in the bed next to me." Her resistance appeared to be wavering.

He grinned. "Hey, if you don't trust yourself, I understand."

She smacked her palms against his chest and wedged some distance between them. "Don't try to use reverse psychology on me."

His fingers trailed along her arm and cupped her elbow. "Would you prefer I use persuasion instead?"

"Why don't you just try asking me to stay?" she challenged.

"I did."

"No, you didn't. You asked me why I was leaving."

He tossed his hands in the air and admitted defeat.

In a war of semantics, she'd nail him every time. "Okay. Will you stay?"

"You said we were starting over, and I never sleep with a man on the first date."

"I only want to have you next to me. Your virtue is safe."

Her deliberately long pause left him holding his breath. Finally she shrugged. "All right. But purely for research purposes. I mean, if I'm going to consider living with you, I should get used to your snoring as well as fighting for the covers and my own space on the bed."

He exhaled slowly. Hooking his finger through her belt loop, he pulled her closer. "Always a smart answer. You couldn't admit that you wanted to stay."

Her enigmatic smile was as infuriating as it was engaging. "I think I'll finish my dinner after all."

He might have gotten what he wanted, but she had by no means given in. He had a long, uphill battle ahead before he regained her trust. Even then, there was no guarantee this wandering Gypsy would ever be able to put down roots.

Sophie packed the last of her belongings in her canvas suitcase and left it at the trailer door. Confusion mingled with a bad case of nerves. What the hell was she doing?

Last night, Alex had kept his word and done nothing more than hold her in his arms—much to her profound disappointment and frustration. Several times, she had deliberately brushed against him while pretending to be asleep. Although she'd felt him respond, he didn't try to alleviate his aroused state. She admired his willpower, especially since she didn't possess any.

She flopped down on a kitchen chair. *Admit it, Sophie. You can't say no to him.* She wanted to. In her heart, she knew they were too different to be able to coexist peacefully. How long before they began to resent each other?

Her past history with relationships hadn't been particularly lucky. She knew all the reasons she should walk away. She also knew that the second she got within ten feet of Alex to tell him, her heart would override any coherent thought in her head. The power he had over her was frightening. She thought about looking into the tarot cards to see what their future held, but she didn't want to know right now. Because deep down she knew she would still follow the same road. With a deep breath for courage, she rose and collected her bags.

Alex ambled along the midway. The carnies were taking down the rides and clearing the fairground. By tomorrow the carnival would be a memory in this small Kansas town. He walked inside Natalie's tent, where he had arranged to meet Sophie.

Natalie was packing her paraphernalia in the large steamer trunk. Without turning to see who had entered, she said, "You're taking Sophie back with you."

"She told you?"

"No."

He no longer wondered how Natalie knew the things she did.

"You don't approve," he noted quietly.

"She doesn't need my permission. She's already made her decision."

"Why do I hear a warning?"

She turned and rested against the trunk with her arms folded across her chest. With her head cocked slightly to one side, she met his gaze. "Do you?"

"You don't like me very much."

"On the contrary, Alex. I'm sure you're a fine man, but I don't think you're right for Sophie. You need to control and she needs to be free."

Sophie had agreed to come home with him. Obviously she was willing to try to make a go of a relationship. "You make it sound like I plan to lock her away."

Natalie tucked her hair behind her ears. "Not intentionally. But there are different kinds of prisons, Alex. You've lived in a few of them yourself."

He tensed at the memories her words inspired. He had lived in many different kinds of prisons. Some had been forced on him, and some were of his own making. But he'd learned from his past and he would give Sophie all the latitude she needed. "Nothing will change except her address."

"As long as you give her space to breathe."

"I'll keep that in mind."

"You better. I might not always have been the best mother, but anyone who messes with my baby lives to regret it."

He grinned. "Fair enough."

"As long as we understand each other."

"What kind of understanding do you have?" Sophie asked as she joined them in the tent. She set her suitcase on the canvas floor.

"All packed?" Natalie asked, smoothly changing the subject.

Sophie's lips formed a wounded pout. "Anxious to get rid of me? Have you got another date, Mama?"

Natalie shook her head and pressed a black onyx amulet into her daughter's hand. "For a safe plane ride. Make sure you call your grandma and give her the phone number. I'll be calling her on Monday."

Sophie patted her mother's back. "You can still reach me through the answering service."

Alex backed away, feeling like an intruder as the two women said goodbye. Despite the unorthodox way she conducted her life, Natalie did love her only child and she had Sophie's best interests at heart.

So did he.

Sophie walked around the L-shaped living room, decorated in contemporary furniture. She knelt on the black leather sofa and gazed out the bay window that overlooked Long Island Sound. Her stomach muscles clenched. She would have preferred going to her apartment first, if only to spend a few hours in familiar surroundings. She was nervous enough and being on Alex's home ground didn't help.

Why did he want her living here? The first time she'd asked, he had given her a vague answer about the correlation between proximity of the parties and building trust. That could also mean he didn't trust her out of his sight. She shook her head. If she began the relationship by expecting the worst, undoubtably that was what she would get.

Alex dropped his keys on the desk. She glanced at his reflection in the glass. His smile warmed her, easing some of her anxiety. That was her problem. Whenever he was around, she forgot all the doubts and misgivings that plagued her when she had time to think rationally instead of hormonally.

"Welcome home," he said.

"It's going to take a while before this feels like home to me." If ever, she silently added.

"Give it time." He came up behind her and slid his hands over her waist. "Why are you tense?"

"I'm not." At least not the kind of tension he was referring to. Her body ached with desire. She wanted him more than she had admitted to him, or herself.

"Do you want to see the rest of the condo?"

She would gladly forgo the sightseeing excursion in favor of a shortcut to the bedroom, but she couldn't bring herself to voice the suggestion. "Okay."

As she started to slip out of his embrace, he tightened his hold. "You don't have to wait for me to ask before you do something. You live here now." He drummed his fingers over her stomach. "What would you be doing if you were in your apartment?"

"That depends." She relaxed against his solid chest. "Are you with me, or am I alone?"

His arm muscles rippled as he cuddled her closer. "I'm there."

"Well, I wouldn't be wasting our time with hypothetical questions."

His hands ran the perimeter of her body. "What are you trying to say?"

She closed her eyes and sighed. "Are you going to make me ask?"

"Yes."

"And if I don't?" she challenged with her last ounce of willpower.

"We can spend another night like last night, where you try to get me turned on while pretending to be asleep."

A warm flush rose in her cheeks. Alex was too smart for his own good and too damn sexy for hers.

With his hands planted firmly on her waist, he turned and dropped into the sofa, pulling her down into his lap. She squirmed around, drawing a groan from him as she brushed against his erection. Before she had time to distract him further, Alex retaliated with his own brand of torture. He slipped his hand under her shirt and palmed her breast. His thumb stroked the pebbled nipple. She jerked in response.

"What's wrong?"

She shook her head. "I don't know. I guess the skin is a little tender there."

He continued to caress her, but more gently. In no time the soreness subsided and pure pleasure took over.

"Tell me what you want, Sophie." His breath fluttered over her neck, uncoiling a ribbon of heat in her belly.

Putting up any resistance would be futile and a waste of time. She needed him as much as she needed her next breath. "You," she muttered on a rush of air. "I want you."

"See how easy that was."

Obviously Alex had no idea how much that admission cost her. His fingers trailed along her stomach, down to the elastic of her shorts. Moisture pooled between her legs; anticipation rose.

She took his hand, guiding him beneath the waistband. His touch was pure magic, pulling her deeper into his seductive spell. He stroked her through the flimsy fabric of her panties until she thought she'd go mad. She arched her back and sighed.

"Impatient," he whispered in her ear. "Maybe I should slow down."

"Don't stop," she squeaked as he started to pull back his hand.

His lips caressed her cheek. "I love it when you get demanding."

She heard the satisfaction in his voice, but she was far beyond caring. Let the man gloat. It had taken him precisely one minute to overcome her challenge and leave her begging for more. "Oh yeah? Then get naked. I want to feel your skin."

A grin settled on his face. "Here, or the bedroom?"

"Here," she muttered. She yanked his Polo shirt off and tossed it carelessly on the floor behind her. "And then the bedroom."

Alex grabbed her wrists and tugged her against his chest. Given half a chance, she would send him right over the edge before she had his clothes off. "You're always in a hurry. Relax. The night is young."

He flicked his tongue over her lips, tasting the strawberry lip gloss. Misty-eyed and breathless, she returned his kiss. Her uninhibited sighs and moans played like a symphony in his mind. He worked her clothing off and settled her beneath him on the sofa.

She wriggled restlessly. "Your jeans," she said on a ragged breath.

"All in good time." He raised himself slightly above her and explored the lines and contours of her body. Damp, pliant and utterly aroused, she arched toward his probing fingers. He flicked his thumb over the sensitive bud at the juncture of her legs. She let out a choked cry.

He felt her tense, fighting to prolong her release. Her lips pursed tightly together, she sucked in several deep breaths. Their foreplay became a contest to see who would give up control first. Sophie possessed a strong and defiant will, but he had the added advantage of clothing.

A barrier she had no trouble working around.

She gripped him firmly, right through the denim fabric, and he swallowed a groan. She showed no mercy as she stroked and squeezed his hard shaft. A jolt of electricity surged though him. He was one second away from conceding defeat when she stopped.

She gazed up at him, her emerald eyes wide and filled with moisture. ''No more games, Alex.'' The intensity in her softly spoken words reverberated in his mind.

Having Sophie with him now, forever, was no game. In truth, he had never been more serious about anything in his life. He would tell her, but he was half-afraid she would bolt like a frightened rabbit.

''Sophie…''

She pressed her mouth to his, while her shaking hands fumbled with the snap on his jeans. There would be time to talk later. Right now, he had one mighty eager woman waiting for him to make love to her. With no hardship to himself, he undertook the endeavor. He knew no faster way to make her feel at home here, with him.

As he entered her, he noted her contented smile. She wanted him, he had no doubt about that. At least, her body did. He had no idea what went through that beautiful head of hers. As much as he liked the idea of making love to her all the time, there had to be more between them if their relationship was to survive.

Sophie let out an impatient squeak and wrapped her legs tighter around his hips. Her eyes implored him to devote his full attention to her. He moved within her, slowly at first as they found a comfortable rhythm. Soon, his misgivings gave way to the pure sensual pleasure of being joined with her. Time stopped and all that mattered was this woman who clung to him and cried out his name.

Twelve

Sophie forced her eyelids open and stared at the ceiling. After ten hours of sleep, she still woke up exhausted. Thankfully Alex had already left for work or he would be on the receiving end of another of her lousy moods. She had attributed her emotional swings of the past month to boredom. Between the cleaning service that came in four days a week, and the fact that they ate out more often than not, Sophie found very little to occupy her day beyond her work. She felt as if she were being *kept*—a rich man's mistress—which was not how she'd envisioned their relationship when she agreed to this arrangement.

Not that Alex had commented on her multiple personalities. He had been so damned agreeable, she wanted to scream. The turnaround from his usual controlling nature would be a surprise if she believed it for a minute. Alex hadn't changed. He almost seemed to be playing a part. But then, so was she. All her words about maintaining her independence, refusing to give up her apartment, were a cover. In truth, she had been fatalistically sure Alex would wake up one day and realize he had made a mistake.

She rolled off the bed and stumbled to the laundry room. Her muscles ached and she felt the start of a cold coming on. That was what she got for walking in the rain last night. She had expected Alex to tell her not to go. When he'd given her his perfunctory shrug, she stubbornly stayed out for three hours. Upon her return, he'd handed her a towel, but didn't make a comment.

Did he already regret asking her to move in? Each day she grew deeper in love and became less sure of him. Why couldn't she get a clear impression of his feelings? What was it about Alex that made him impossible to read?

She pulled her Levi's from the dryer and wandered into the living room. The aroma of coffee lingered in the air. As she struggled into her snug jeans, she had to deal with a worry she'd been trying to deny. Queasy stomach, fatigue and mood swings that would do her Romany heritage proud—this was no cold coming on. Add to that the fact that her period was two weeks late and she could only conclude that she was pregnant. Her body trembled anxiously. A baby. Alex's baby. What would the news do to their already precarious relationship?

She hopped several times while tugging at the waistband of the jeans and wrenched up the zipper. With a sigh, she smoothed her T-shirt over her hips. Slightly breathless, she leaned against the arm of the sofa. A warm tingle washed over her. That could only mean one thing. She turned slowly and found Alex sitting in a chair in the dining room watching her with a grin.

"Nice little dance number."

He looked incredibly sexy in his charcoal gray suit. And even better out of it, she recalled. If she weren't so tired, she would refresh her memory. "I thought you were at work."

"I had a few things to take care of first." He rose and walked into the living room. "You look pale."

"You scared me," she offered feebly.

"No, I didn't. You knew I was there. You always do." He brushed at a strand of hair sticking to her damp cheek.

"I'm probably coming down with a cold."

She waited for him to lecture her about her stroll in the rain, but he didn't comment. "Would you like me to take you to a doctor?"

Undoubtedly, she should see a doctor, but not with Alex. She couldn't bear it if he felt obligated to *do the right thing*. Or worse, if he jumped to the conclusion that she had deliberately gotten pregnant as part of Damon's master scheme. It wouldn't be the first time he'd made that leap. Although, to be fair, he had apologized for his off-base accusation. "I'll be fine."

A spark of anger flashed in his eyes. His jaw locked in determination, and he looked as if he was about to insist.

"What?" she said, pushing.

He shrugged his shoulders casually. "Nothing."

Frustration ran through her. Again he had backed down. Before she could push him for an answer, the doorbell rang. "That's probably for you. I'm going to take a shower."

Alex watched until she disappeared down the hall. The woman would be the death of him. For the past couple of weeks she had been irritable and tired. Walking in the rain at midnight was only the last in a series of ridiculous stunts she had pulled. Overly conscious about invading her space, he had kept his opinions to himself. Although not without difficulty. If she was pushing him into a fight, eventually she was going to get one. He couldn't take much more.

Was she unhappy living with him? The bell rang again. With a groan, he strode across the room and opened the door. He glanced at Damon's arrogant face and let out several expletives.

"What do you want?"

Undaunted, Damon grinned. "Are you going to let me in?"

Alex stepped aside and allowed Damon to enter. His stepbrother made himself right at home in the reclining seat.

"What can I do for you? I have to get to work."

"I got a letter from your attorney. He said you got an offer on the house."

"I know," Alex said. "I had him send it."

"Does that mean you plan to sell?"

"Yes. Is that all you wanted?"

Damon arched a brow in confusion and leaned forward in the chair. "I thought it was about what *you* wanted. I take it you couldn't find Sophie on your own."

Alex rested on the arm of the sofa and folded his arms over his chest. "You know where she is?"

"I have the address."

"Bleeker Street, but she doesn't live there any-more." Although, to Alex's irritation, she continued to pay the rent.

Damon's jaw sagged. "She's probably with her mother for a few weeks, but she'll be back."

"She's not with her mother. Or did you think I wouldn't know how to track down the carnival on my own?"

Damon cracked his knuckles as if trying to relieve tension. "Is that going to affect the sale?"

Alex let out a bitter laugh. "Always worried about yourself. No, it doesn't affect the sale. The sooner, the better, as far as I'm concerned."

"I could check with some of her friends—"

"Alex, do you have any…" Sophie came into the room and stopped short when she saw Damon. Beads of water shone on her arms and legs. Her wet hair dripped onto her oversize T-shirt, which clung in strategic places to her damp body. Alex wasn't sure who looked more stunned—Damon or Sophie.

She pressed her hand to her stomach. "I think I'm going to be sick." Pivoting on her heel, she darted to the bathroom.

"Morning sickness?" Damon joked.

Alex wasn't amused. "I'd say she wasn't pleased to see you."

"How long has she been living here?"

Alex shoved his hands in his pockets. "You've never had any interest in my life unless it was to screw it up. Don't start now. I'll have the lawyer inform you of the closing date."

Damon puffed up indignantly, but apparently thought better of making an equally nasty retort. "Is she all right?"

"Do you care?"

He hunched his shoulders and made his way toward the door. "Actually, I do." In his own, twisted, self-centered way, Damon probably did care. He'd lost a good friend in Sophie.

"I'm sure she'll be fine. Tell Elaine she can take whatever she wants from the house. We'll auction the rest."

"What about the horses?"

"I've already found a place for them."

Damon half grinned. "I'm glad that things worked out between you and Sophie."

"Had it ever occurred to you to just come ask me about borrowing from the trust to buy the club in Soho? Or was it more important that you get me out of your life?"

Damon's jaw sagged in surprise. "You know about that? What would you have said?"

"I probably would have said yes, if it was a good investment."

"It is."

"I hope so, because once that trust is divided, you'll get exactly what you want. And I'll be out of your life."

Once Damon left, Alex made his way to the bathroom to check on Sophie. Her color had returned, and her eyes had lost the glassy sheen.

He cupped his hand over her waist. "I think you hurt his feelings."

"Damon? How?"

"You really looked like you were going to be sick."

"I thought I was. I wouldn't run away from a confrontation.'' She poured a glass of water from the tap. ''Social visit?''

''Oh, yeah. He's real brotherly now that he knows I'm selling the house.''

''You're selling?'' Her voice pitched in surprise and sorrow.

''I thought you hated The Sanctuary.''

''It's your home. You shouldn't sell the place if you like it.''

''It's not my home anymore.'' He slid his hand across her stomach. He noticed her tense before she could stop herself. ''You really are sick.''

''Must be the pizza I ate last night.'' She fidgeted with the bottom of her T-shirt and avoided his gaze. An uncomfortable silence hung between them. She was hiding something from him.

Perhaps Damon's crack about morning sickness wasn't off-base. Could she be pregnant? He thought back over the past month. All the signs were there. Tired, irritable, upset stomach. Anger caused all his muscles to tense. How long had she known? Was she planning to tell him? His fingers clenched into fists.

''Why don't you lie down for a while?''

''Later. I have an idea for the Prentiss job, and I want to try it out.''

''Sophie, I really think you should...''

She raised her chin defiantly. ''Yes?''

Alex sucked in a large gulp of air. Losing his temper right now would be counterproductive. He needed a plan of attack before he battled her. He dropped his hand. ''I'll see you later.''

''Alex?'' She swayed into him. Her fingers grasped his suit jacket. ''I think I'd better lie down.''

He lifted her into his arms. "What a good idea. Why didn't I think of that?" he grumbled under his breath.

Damn her! How long did she think she would be able to keep this from him?

He carried her to the bedroom and placed her on the bed. She curled around a pillow and squeezed her eyes shut, looking thoroughly miserable. And a lucky thing for her she did, or he'd give her an earful. He had been dancing around the subject of their future for over a month now because he didn't want her to feel pressured. But her refusal to give up her apartment had rankled him. It was as if she was waiting for their relationship to fail.

When she felt better, they had to have a serious talk about where they were heading. No way would he let his child grow up without a father the way she had. If that meant she had to give up some of her precious independence and depend on him for help, then she would just have to learn how to deal with it.

Thirteen

———

Sophie twirled the straw in the glass of ginger ale she had been nursing for the past hour. Her first evening out with her friends since she had moved in with Alex and she couldn't even enjoy herself. Perhaps it had been cowardly to leave a message on Alex's voice mail, but he had been tied up in meetings all day and hadn't been able to come to the phone.

He would probably welcome the break, she decided. Lately he seemed to be on edge around her. Sometimes he hovered, reminding her that they had a cleaning service if she tried to vacuum the carpet or wash a floor. Other times he would just stare at her without saying a word. Since Damon's visit the other day, their sex life had become a memory. Did Alex resent her for his decision to sell his home? She thought about asking him if he wanted her to leave but, in truth, she was afraid of the answer.

She glanced across the bar. Her friends, enjoying the company of a trio of handsome men, had forgotten all about her. She slumped into the seat and listened to the folksinger crooning ballads from the sixties. The acoustic guitar sounded hauntingly sad. Or maybe her mood was melancholy.

Her hand automatically went to her stomach. She had taken one of those home pregnancy tests to be sure, although she hadn't worked up the nerve to mention her condition to Alex. She started to on several occasions, but she couldn't shake the feeling that she would be using her condition as a means to hold him. Would he feel the same way?

"Is this seat taken?"

Before she could give her standard "I'm waiting for my husband" line that kept men away, she caught sight of Damon's grinning face. "What do you want?"

"Are you feeling better today?" he asked with what seemed like genuine concern, but she wasn't in a forgiving mood.

"I was until you sat down," she grumbled. "I thought you didn't go out before sundown."

"We stopped by for dinner." He gestured toward his friends at the bar. "I didn't expect to find you here. Is Alex meeting you?"

"I thought you didn't like this place." She had agreed to meet her friends at the downtown dinner club because she felt sure Damon wouldn't come to the local hangout. The small restaurant wasn't flashy enough for his tastes.

"It's all right for a change. I left a couple of messages for you, but you haven't returned any of my calls."

"Are you surprised?"

"Hey, everything worked out in the end."

"So you figured all's well that ends well? Let me tell you, your *stepbrother* is a bigger person than I am. If it were up to me, I would have held on to that house until I was old and gray."

Damon shrugged off her comment. "Speaking of Alex, where is he?"

"Home."

"He let you out?"

He let her do whatever she damn well pleased. No matter how she tried to goad him into a showdown, he backed off. Or he didn't care enough to fight. The thought made her frown.

"You didn't tell him you were going out?" Damon asked, misreading her expression.

"I'm not going to discuss Alex with you. Go back to your pals and leave me to mine."

He shot a glance toward her friends. "They appear to be otherwise engaged. Will you be able to get back to Stamford tonight?"

Damon's show of concern came too late. "I'll manage." She had been getting around on her own for years. As long as she left before ten, she would make it back before midnight.

"If you need a ride later..." His words trailed off as he rose from the seat. "Take care."

She nodded and watched as he retreated to the far end of the bar. For another hour and a half, she remained alone at the table, freezing off any man who approached with an icy stare. The sun hadn't even set for the evening and she was bored to death. What good was making a point if she made herself miserable in the process? She might as well admit that she'd rather be with Alex, no matter what his mood, and go home.

Just the thought of him brought a familiar tingling sensation. She closed her eyes and enjoyed the moment until she realized the implication. Alex was nearby.

"Come on. Time to leave."

Sophie raised her head and gazed at Alex's thunderous face. Although she'd felt his presence, she still couldn't believe her eyes. She blinked. "How did you know I was here?"

"Damon called. He was afraid you would be foolish enough to take the train back alone. Get your things. We're going."

She arched her eyebrows. "We are?"

Alex dropped some money on the table for the waitress's tip, then cupped his fingers around her forearm. "I'll make a scene if you want."

"No. That won't be necessary." She settled her purse strap on her shoulder and allowed him to lead her to his car, parked a few blocks away.

For several minutes they sat in silence. Alex gripped the wheel in a white-knuckled grasp. The darkening sky loomed through the windshield, complementing his mood.

"Are you going to talk to me?" she finally asked.

"Not in the car," he let out through clenched teeth.

"Why?" she pushed.

"Because I'm mad as hell right now."

"Well, it's about time," she snapped. She settled deep in the bucket seat and crossed one stocking-clad leg over the other, causing her short skirt to rise even higher. The movement was purely provocative and momentarily distracted him. When he noticed Sophie unconsciously rub her hand over her stomach, his anger returned.

He had never lost his temper with a woman before, but he was a hairbreadth away from exploding right now. Not that he cared if she wanted to spend time with her friends, but she had been sick for the past three days. Her first day on her feet, she ran out the door an hour before he was due home from work. If Damon hadn't called, he'd still be pacing the floor wondering where she went. It was the only considerate act his stepbrother had ever performed.

How could she be so foolish? And in her condition?

He jammed the car into gear and negotiated the crowded streets. The Friday traffic leaving the city did little to cool his temper. By the time he reached the condo, he knew Sophie was going to get the fight she so dearly wanted.

Alex paced the carpet of the living room with long, graceful strides. Tension blanketed the still room. Sophie sat in the wing chair with her feet tucked underneath her. The ride home from the city had been the longest hour of her life. She wished he would just explode and get it over with. His damned control was unnatural.

He turned slowly toward her. "This isn't working, Sophie."

His words impacted with the force of a train. A suffocating weight settled over her heart. The conversation she had feared the past few weeks was one she could no longer avoid. She folded her arms across her stomach, finding a small measure of comfort from the one part of Alex she would never lose.

"I know."

Alex lowered himself into the sofa across from her. Resting his elbows on his knees, he leaned forward. His expression was unreadable. "I can't live like this. You were right. I need control. I've tried to give you all the latitude you need, but it's killing me."

She twisted her fingers together in her lap. "I've tried every way I know to get you to stop."

"I realize that." He expelled a deep groan of frustration. "I mean, I don't care if you want to spend time with your friends."

"I didn't really want to," she admitted quietly. Nothing from her old life appealed to her anymore. Not the clubs, not the hectic pace of the city, and especially not living alone.

Alex rolled his eyes. "It's nice to know you'd do anything to get away from me."

"Well, I figured you wanted a break from me."

For a long moment he regarded her in silence. A lump formed in her throat, threatening to choke her.

"Why aren't you happy here?" he finally asked.

The denial on her lips remained unspoken. She wouldn't take all the blame for their problems. They were still role-playing with each other instead of being themselves. "I don't want to be your mistress, Alex."

His jaw tightened and golden sparks flashed in his eyes. "What does that mean?"

Too nervous to sit any longer, she pushed to her feet. "I don't do anything. The cleaning service does all the housework. Obviously you don't care for my cooking since we eat out five nights a week. You pay all the bills. The only thing I contribute is my body, and lately you aren't particularly interested in me that way."

He chuckled. "Three days is hardly a dry spell."

Her temper rose. She had just bared her soul and he was laughing at her! "It proves there's a problem."

"Well, that's apparent."

"I told you I wasn't a good roommate." She stared out the window at the murky water. He sat less than three feet away, but the distance between them felt like miles.

"I don't want a roommate, Sophie."

The air left her lips in a rush. She felt numb. "Well, then I guess it's a good thing I haven't given up my apartment."

"Excuse me?"

"It shouldn't take me long to pack my stuff and

get out of here.'' Chin held high, she started for the bedroom. She might as well begin packing.

Alex caught up to her in the hall. Apparently they had their signals crossed. ''What are you talking about?''

''Moving out.''

Moisture pooled in her eyes. Although he hated to see her cry, the display of emotion was probably a good sign.

He brushed his thumb over her tearstained cheek. ''Are we speaking the same language here? I don't want you to leave.''

She arched a delicate eyebrow skeptically. ''You said it wasn't working.''

''That doesn't mean we pack it in. We talk it out. Like beginning with what you expected when you moved in with me?''

''I thought... I figured... Forget it.'' Her body trembled. ''You'll think I'm an idiot.''

''I need to know.''

She ran her tongue across her lip. He longed to kiss the worry from her mouth, but until he knew the problem, she wasn't likely to accept his solution.

''I figured I would do my work during the day. When you came home, I'd make dinner, we'd hang out in our underwear and complain about how lousy the day was, then we'd watch some TV and make love. Sounds stupid, right?''

Had he been wrong in letting her do as she pleased without comment? He had, in effect, treated her like a roommate, and apparently given her the wrong impression about what he wanted from the relationship.

Which was a hell of a lot more than he'd demanded. "That sounds a lot like marriage, Sophie."

She shrugged. "I wouldn't really know. It's not a big tradition in my family."

Her eyes shimmered with sadness and unspent tears. Could it be that Miss Independence was really a homebody, after all? "What about your Gypsy need for freedom? Giving you your space?"

"Did I ever tell you I felt crowded by you?"

"No," he admitted. Those ideas came from people who apparently didn't know Sophie at all. He had wanted to make her happy, so he had trusted the advice rather than following his instincts.

"Did I ask you to change who you are?"

"I thought you said I was too controlling."

"You are. But I knew how to handle you. At least I thought I did, but lately you don't seem to give a damn what I do."

His jaw went slack. She should only know how many times he had wanted to shake some sense into her. "Is that what you think?"

"I've been trying to get your attention and all you do is blow me off."

"You want to fight?"

"Of course. It's healthy in a relationship. Why do you think I've been spoiling for one?"

He slid his hand across her back and anchored her against his chest. She felt so right in his arms. Sophie was his family, and he wasn't about to let her go. "I figured your hormones were jumping, and you weren't responsible for your actions."

"What kind of a sexist remark is that?" she grunted indignantly.

"Isn't that what happens to pregnant women?"

Her eyes widened and she let out a gasp. He tightened his hold as she tried to pull away.

"How did you know?"

"It doesn't take a genius. Morning sickness. You've been murder to live with. And you haven't had your period since you've been here."

She lowered her head and mumbled, "I didn't think you'd noticed."

"I notice everything about you." He raked his fingers into her hair, raising her head until she met his gaze. "Why didn't you talk to me about it?"

"I was scared." She swallowed hard as if her throat was parched.

"What did you think I'd do? Walk out on you and leave my child to grow up without a father?"

"No." Her denial came swiftly, but in light of her family history, he felt sure the possibility went through her mind.

"Then why didn't you tell me?"

"I didn't want you to feel trapped. I don't expect you to marry me."

His fingers spanned the width of her stomach where their baby was growing inside her. A river of pride and protectiveness washed over him. "Too bad, because that's exactly what I plan to do."

Her body went rigid. She pressed her hands against his chest and pushed him back. "This is precisely what I was afraid of."

She brushed past him and sprinted into the bedroom. He followed.

"What were you afraid of?"

With a dramatic sigh, she dropped down on the bed. "That you would do the right thing. I don't want to marry you because I'm pregnant."

He towered above her. "That's not why I want to marry you."

"Then why?"

He let out a groan of exasperation. "I would have thought it was obvious. I love you."

"You do?" she asked suspiciously.

"Yes." He sat on the bed next to her. The delicate scent of apricot that had been driving him slowly insane the past few nights wafted around him. "Am I wrong in thinking you love me, too?"

"No."

"Then say it."

"I love you." Her words came out in a choked whisper. She cleared her throat and tried again. "I love you."

Relief ran through him like a fever. He kissed her parted lips, tasting a mix of minty sweetness and salty tears. She deepened the kiss, arching closer. The need for more rose in him and he reluctantly, and not without great effort, drew back. Now was not the time.

A flash of hurt lit her emerald eyes.

"You believe I love you, don't you?"

She raised a half smile. "I guess."

Her words lacked conviction. He couldn't blame her entirely. From the moment he'd laid eyes on her, he had felt drawn to her. By the time they had consummated their relationship in the stables, he was already in love. Yet he had allowed past experiences to cloud what should have been obvious. No wonder she had trouble believing him now.

Still, she had always known when he was around, as if he were a part of her right from the start. "For a woman who gets really strong impressions about people, why do you find it so difficult to know what I'm feeling for you?"

"I've never been able to read you. The physical pull was so strong, it seemed to obliterate everything else." As she cuddled around a pillow, he figured she must be exhausted. He stroked her hair until she purred.

"Why don't you get some rest now and we'll finish this tomorrow?"

"I don't want to sleep, Alex. I want to make love."

Not any more than he did, though he was surprised by her request. He stretched out on the bed alongside her and rested his hand on her belly. "What about the baby?"

"What about him?" Her mouth dropped open. "Is that why you haven't touched me?"

He grinned sheepishly. "And it hasn't been easy."

She exhaled a sigh of relief, then broke out in a smile so bright his heart skipped a beat. "I thought you were bored with me."

He had been infuriated, exasperated and sometimes plain confused by her, but never bored. "I was afraid I might hurt you."

"Well, get over it. You won't hurt me or the baby. Although I can't guarantee my well-being if you plan to keep your distance for the next eight months." She wrapped her arms around his neck and pulled him on top of her.

"Don't you think we should talk about the wedding first?"

She wriggled beneath him, twisting with provocative purpose. "Not right now," she muttered impatiently.

He wasn't sure if she wanted to avoid the subject or if, like him, she was just feeling hot and aroused. Perhaps a little of both. Nothing he could say would fully convince her that marriage was his intention all along. However, he did have something to show her that might do the trick. He gazed down at her face, glowing with desire and anticipation. Maybe now wasn't the best time.

Tomorrow.

Alex maneuvered the Bronco down the winding road that seemed vaguely familiar to Sophie. All morning long, he had been acting strangely. She had expected him to start right in on wedding plans, but he hadn't even mentioned the subject. After breakfast, when she tried to entice him back into bed, he'd announced that they had afternoon plans. Having selfishly kept him up half the night, she decided in good conscience that he deserved a break.

As they headed north on I-25, she figured they were going to The Sanctuary, but he insisted they weren't. Beyond that, he'd volunteered no information. When he pulled off the main road, she caught sight of the farmhouse they had visited together.

"What are we doing here?" she asked.

He cut the engine and opened his door. "Come on. I want to show you something."

As they walked together across the grassy lawn, she noticed the Sold sign hanging on the fence that surrounded the paddock. A horse sprinted over to the gate.

"He looks like Elvis," she said.

"He is."

"What's going on?" She gazed at Alex. A Cheshire-cat grin covered his face. "Did you buy this place?"

"Close. *We're* buying this place."

"What?"

He took her hand and led her to the house. "I rented until the closing. We're going to get a mortgage, a deed, a joint bank account. Yours and mine. His and hers. Understand?"

She tipped her head. The implication that he wanted her as his wife, not his mistress, wasn't lost on her.

Inside, the house had been decorated with the furniture from her apartment. Atop the fireplace mantel sat the knickknacks and collectibles that had made her feel at home no matter where she lived. "When did you do all this?"

"When we got back from Kansas. Of course, I only recently moved your furniture after I made an offer and signed a lease. I can't go to contract without your signature."

Alex had wanted to marry her before he even knew about the baby. Happiness bubbled within her. "A house?"

He nodded. She felt the excitement, and anxiety, radiating from him. It was the clearest impression she had ever gotten from him.

"I thought the guest cottage would make a good office for you. You've got all the space you could ever need."

"True."

"So, what do you think?"

"I love the house."

"I mean about getting married and raising our family here?"

"Are you sure this is what you want?"

"Very."

Strangely, she had no more doubts. She wanted a life with Alex and their children more than anything else in the world. Loving him gave her all the freedom she needed. And for the first time since meeting Alex, she knew exactly what was in his heart. He loved her completely and without reservation.

She gazed up at him and smiled. "All right. Just as long as you realize marriage is forever."

"I wouldn't have it any other way."

*   *   *   *   *

Watch for rising star Kathryn Taylor's
next Silhouette Desire® title,
THE SCANDALOUS HEIRESS,
available in January 2000.

SILHOUETTE
DESIRE ®

AVAILABLE FROM 22ND OCTOBER 1999

LOVE ME TRUE Ann Major

Man of the Month

Joey Fasano had wealth, fame and success. But when he saw his old flame Heather Wade he realized his life was incomplete, especially as the child whose hand she was holding was his spitting image!

HER HOLIDAY SECRET Jennifer Greene

Maggie Fletcher remembered everything except the past twenty-four hours. Luckily for her, cop Andy Gautier could get to the bottom of anything—even a woman with some long-repressed desires…

THE DADDY AND THE BABY DOCTOR Kristin Morgan

Follow That Baby

Sam Arquette wanted information about one of Amanda Lucas's patients—and he made it clear he also wanted her. Amanda couldn't break a patient's confidence—but could she resist this sexy single dad?

THE LAW AND GINNY MARLOW Marie Ferrarella

The Cutler Family

When Ginny Marlow stormed into Sheriff Quint Cutler's office to bail out her little sister, she didn't expect to be sentenced herself—or that the man who'd thrown her in jail was her future husband!

THE COWBOY WHO CAME IN FROM THE COLD
Pamela Macaluso

Rugged, seductive Stone Garret was offering Patrice Caldwell shelter from the storm raging outside. He was also tempting her to find comfort in his arms after her fiancé had betrayed her…

HART'S BABY Christy Lockhart

When Cassie Morrison arrived on Zach Hart's doorstep with a baby, he assumed she was after the family fortune. But soon it didn't matter whether or not the baby was really a Hart, he wanted them both to be his.

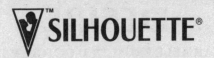

4 FREE

books and a surprise gift!

We would like to take this opportunity to thank you for reading this Silhouette® book by offering you the chance to take FOUR more specially selected titles from the Desire™ series absolutely FREE! We're also making this offer to introduce you to the benefits of the Reader Service™—

- ★ FREE home delivery
- ★ FREE gifts and competitions
- ★ FREE monthly Newsletter
- ★ Exclusive Reader Service discounts
- ★ Books available before they're in the shops

Accepting these FREE books and gift places you under no obligation to buy, you may cancel at any time, even after receiving your free shipment. Simply complete your details below and return the entire page to the address below. *You don't even need a stamp!*

YES! Please send me 4 free Desire books and a surprise gift. I understand that unless you hear from me, I will receive 6 superb new titles every month for just £2.70 each, postage and packing free. I am under no obligation to purchase any books and may cancel my subscription at any time. The free books and gift will be mine to keep in any case.

D9EA

Ms/Mrs/Miss/Mr ....Initials..................................
BLOCK CAPITALS PLEASE

Surname ....

Address ....

....

....Postcode..................................

Send this whole page to:
UK: FREEPOST CN81, Croydon, CR9 3WZ
EIRE: PO Box 4546, Kilcock, County Kildare (stamp required)

SHARON Sala

He knows more than any innocent
man should…

Gabriel Donner has been experiencing
disturbing dreams of horrible murders, dreams
that mean he knows details of the murders
the police don't yet know.
Will they believe he is innocent
or does he know too much?

Reunion